ROARING ACRES

ROARING ACRES

A WESTERN STORY

L. P. HOLMES

FIVE STAR

An imprint of Thomson Gale, a part of The Thomson Corporation

Detroit • New York • San Francisco • New Haven, Conn. • Waterv

THOMSON
GALE

LIBRARY OF CONGRESS CATALOGING-IN-PUBLICATION DATA

Holmes, L. P. (Llewellyn Perry), 1895–
  Roaring acres : a western story / by L.P. Holmes. — 1st ed.
   p. cm.
  ISBN-13: 978-1-59414-626-8 (alk. paper)
  ISBN-10: 1-59414-626-8 (alk. paper)
  1. Frontier and pioneer life—Fiction. I. Title.
PS3515.O4448R627 2007
813'.52—dc22   2007010707

First Edition. First Printing: July 2007.

Published in 2007 in conjunction with Golden West Literary Agency.

Printed in the United States of America on permanent paper
10 9 8 7 6 5 4 3 2 1

Roaring Acres

CHAPTER ONE

Once he had finished the last bit of business in Stony Ford, Dave Salkeld turned his back on all of that burned, heat-blasted, drought-cursed range with a certain air of finality. In the past year and a half of bitter struggle against hostile conditions, he had grown to hate this country. He never wanted to see it again.

He rode fast through the waning hours of the afternoon, heading southwest. Comparatively late in the day though it was, sodden heat was still there. The bronco he was on was tough and wiry, yet, even so, rolls of dirty foam were gathered about the edges of Salkeld's saddle blanket. Sweat coursed down the lean, hard planes of his own face, glistened on the corded bronze of his throat, and his shirt clung, darkly wet, to the wide, flat sweep of his shoulders. Hat pulled low, right shoulder hunched against the relentless smash of the sun, Salkeld rode the afternoon out and hailed the dusty, blue dusk with a curse of relief.

If Salkeld's calculations were right, he ought to catch up with Buck Custer and the Flying Diamond herd somewhere around Tunison Wells. Buck Custer, Salkeld's partner, had gone on ahead with the herd, leaving Salkeld to clean up the last business items about Stony Ford.

Salkeld had to chuckle when he thought of how effectively he had done the job. They had known from the first that penny-pinching old Frenchy DuBois had long wanted to get his hands on the former holdings of the Flying Diamond on the Stony

Ford range. When Salkeld had gone to DuBois with the offer to sell, DuBois had tried to drive a hard bargain, knowing that the Flying Diamond was pulling out for the new country that the government was going to open in Gallatin Basin. Salkeld hadn't wasted any time arguing with that old pelican. He had stated his price and told DuBois to take it or leave it, else he and Custer were prepared to give the range to Frank Connors. DuBois had put up a wail like a wounded coyote, but in the end he met Salkeld's price. He had the money for that sale safely tucked away in his saddlebags.

All night, Salkeld rode. Around midnight he threaded through the gaunt desolation that was the Burned Hills. Beyond them the night was magically cooler. Weariness dropped from bronco and rider and the pace speeded up.

He crossed the sinks south of the Burned Hills and breasted the long, rising slope of the mesa country beyond. The first gray streak of dawn crept out of the east when he topped that slope and moved out across the mesa proper. Only a few miles now, to Tunison Wells.

Salkeld threw another glance to the east. The sun was still a good hour away. Tomorrow, at this time, thousands of eyes would be watching that eastern horizon, measuring time with mounting eagerness, waiting for the first gleam of the sun. For sunrise tomorrow was jump-off time, the official moment for the start of the land rush into Gallatin Basin. The start would be from the Navajo River Meadows, and he'd be there, waiting for the sun with all the rest of them.

A distant murmur reached Salkeld's ears, the complaint of weary cattle being stirred from a bedding ground, to face another day of travel. A hard grin touched Salkeld's lips. Buck Custer had the Flying Diamond herd at Tunison Wells, sure enough. Good old Buck! A man to tie to.

The mesa threw a low crest just ahead and Salkeld was

halfway up it when a medley of faint sounds jerked his head up, taut and alert. Shrill, high yells, the flat *thudding* of guns, and an abrupt change in the sound of the herd. That peaceful, weary plaint took on a hoarse and startled rumble, a note of fear. Salkeld gigged his bronco sharply and sent that weary animal lunging for the crest.

Beyond lay a wide, flat swale, a good half mile across. Near the center was the herd, a great, dark blanket in the mists that still clung to the hollow. That dark blanket of cattle was moving in one solid mass down on the crimson eye of a campfire. Even as Salkeld watched, the movement of the herd speeded up, faster—faster. Those cattle were running. Something had set the herd off. This was stampede!

Salkeld drove his pony, lunging down into the swale. A dozen thoughts jerked through his mind. The herd was running straight at that campfire. Buck Custer and the other boys would be around the fire. They might get caught, trampled. If the herd kept running the way it was headed, it would end up in a stretch of *malpais* country over west where all hell and the devil himself couldn't rout them out of inside a couple of weeks of killing work.

These were some of the thoughts that flashed in Salkeld's mind. And one other. The herd hadn't started to run for no reason at all. Something definite had set them off. And that something might be. . . .

He saw it then, a pale fluttering along the edge of the surging, crazed herd. Salkeld, biting out a bitter curse, spurred that way. As he rode, he slid a naked gun into one taut fist.

A running herd of this size was living thunder. It had a sound all its own, a deep, ominous rolling sound, that froze a man's heart and laid slivers of ice along his spine. A sound that, once heard, would never be forgotten. It had destruction in it, the heavy snarl of flood waters, the ponderous rumble of a landslide.

It dwarfed all sound of Salkeld's hard-riding approach. So it was that the first of the two men who were spurring up and down along the eastern fringe of the herd, yelling and waving yellow slickers, was unaware of Salkeld's arrival until Salkeld was within short yards of him. Then he saw and understood. He dropped the slicker, cursing, and clawed frantically for a gun. Salkeld, without slowing his headlong pace, shot the fellow through the body, twice. The rider was already falling from his saddle as Salkeld sped by, heading for that second slicker-waving figure.

Heavy as was the rumble of the stampede, the reports of Salkeld's gun had cut through, and the other rider had heard and understood. He dropped his slicker, whirled his horse, and raced away. Salkeld went after him, spurring mercilessly.

There was no halfway ground on which to meet renegades like these two. You went after them and you got them, if you could. Salkeld measured the distance through the misty dawn and saw that he was outhorsed. The long miles he had covered through the night had taken all the edge off his own bronco. That fleeing rider was pulling away.

Salkeld sat up to a sliding halt, leaped from the saddle, dragging at the rifle slung in a scabbard under his near saddle fender. He jammed the lever back and forth, dropped to one knee.

The light was bad. The sights blurred against the bobbing figure heading so frantically for the haven of mists. Salkeld held low and cut loose, twice. At the second shot that racing horse went high in the air with a wild, stricken lunge and came down crashing, throwing its rider headlong.

The fellow got to his feet, weaving dazedly. He was shooting back at Salkeld now, but his lead was wild. Salkeld held low, almost at the fellow's feet, making allowance for course sighting. The recoil of the rifle swayed Salkeld's shoulder back. He heard the bullet tell, with a flat, sodden *thud*. The target jackknifed at the waist, and then was only a tiny blot of shadow on the earth. Salkeld went back into the saddle and whirled after the herd.

It had drawn away from him somewhat, but was as yet still short of full speed. The west edge of the herd had not known the terror of those waving slickers and, with the weariness of the drive still in it, moved with a certain reluctance, still bearing back against the pressure from the rear. But this was only a temporary thing. Given a few moments more time the blind fever of the stampede would carry these herd leaders away and they would let go full out.

Of course, there were other obstacles up front now. Mounted men. Men who had gained saddles just in time, before the living flood had flowed over the ground where they had slept, over the fire they had been gathered about to eat their frugal breakfast. These men were putting out superhuman effort to keep the stampede under control, to keep it from getting entirely away from them. Up and down they spurred, slashing rope ends across sullen bovine faces, yelling, shooting in the air—anything to hold that herd back.

But it was beginning to be a losing fight. Slowly and remorselessly the speed of the herd picked up, ponderous and overwhelming.

Salkeld was riding like a madman, down the north flank of the herd. His hard-run pony seemed to understand the urgency, for from somewhere it gathered a new burst of speed and strength. Well up toward the point, Salkeld began bearing in on the speeding cattle, rope end flailing. It was the only chance. You couldn't stop a running herd by frontal pressure. You had to press in at the side, gradually turning the leaders, forcing them to swing away into the start of a circle. Once this maneuver was fully accomplished, the crazed cattle would continue running in a blind circle until exhaustion rose greater than initial terror, and the brutes would stop of their own accord.

That was the theory. But the practice of it was another story. Salkeld could not feel that he was making an inch of progress. It was like trying to turn a raging flood with a handful of sand. Twice, in the fury of his efforts, Salkeld's pony stumbled and nearly went down. That would have been instantly fatal to both horse and rider.

A big, burly whiteface steer, running blind crazy, drove a shoulder into Salkeld's horse, lifting the gallant pony yards to one side. Salkeld, in a burst of fury, threw down and shot the rampaging brute dead. When he saw the other cattle instinctively sheer away from the dead animal, Salkeld dropped another, a little closer in.

The herd sheered farther to the left. Salkeld knew his first glimmer of hope. He drove his mount recklessly in, using his rope end with all his strength.

Up ahead, alert eyes had noticed this slight shift of the cattle and a moment later there were two riders barging in beside Salkeld, adding the pressure of their ropes and mounts to his. That left turn grew. More riders appeared, added their weight to the battle.

Slowly but surely the herd swung farther and farther to the left, and the yelling, rope-wielding riders kept pace with it, always keeping that pressure on. Now the leaders of the herd were breasting a long, low slope and, when riders got above them, willingly turned away from the hard lift of the rise, sped parallel with it for a time, then swung downhill again. And then those laboring riders whooped with relief.

Theory had become fact. The herd was circling now. The leaders were speeding after the drag, the drag blindly following the leaders. There was nothing further to do now but let the herd run itself out. The brutes wouldn't go anywhere. They would end up right where they began, gasping, wild-eyed, exhausted.

A rider came racing up to Salkeld, as he pulled aside to let his shaking, exhausted mount rest. It was Buck Custer. "Dave!" he yelled. "When in hell . . . how . . . ?"

"I got here just as the cattle started to run, Buck," explained Dave wearily. "And it wasn't a pipe dream that set them off, either."

"I've been wondering about that," growled Custer savagely. "I heard those first yells and shots, and once I thought I got a glimpse of a waving slicker."

"You did." Salkeld nodded. "There were two of them. I got 'em both. One was Mink Shroeder."

"Mink Shroeder!" spat Custer. "That means . . . Luke Converse schemed this thing. Luke Converse!"

"Who else?" Salkeld shrugged. "Any of our boys get caught?"

"Don't believe so," said Custer. "I'll check up."

He spurred away, calling to his men. Salkeld tried to build a smoke. He spilled half a sack of tobacco before he succeeded. His hands were shaking; he was shaking all over with weariness. He was ready to drop. He slid out of the saddle and sprawled flat on his back on the cool, dew-moistened earth. He felt he'd like to sleep for a week. Only he could not have slept just now. His nerves were jumping too badly. This thing had been close—too close.

Custer came back, dismounted, and dropped beside Salkeld. "All safe and accounted for. They're getting all around those fool cattle, making sure that circle stays complete. And the herd is slowing down."

Salkeld could tell that by the sound. He lay with eyes closed. "Buck," he said, "I reckon you'll agree with what I've claimed all along, now. There is no place on any range for the Flying Diamond and Luke Converse at the same time. That fellow fights dirty. Had the herd got away from us, we'd have had one devil of a job getting it out of that *malpais*. It would have put us 'way behind time, 'way off our schedule. It might have blown all our plans higher than a busted kite. Make no mistake about it . . . Converse figured things that way."

Custer nodded. "You're right, Dave. I was hoping that Gallatin Basin would be plenty big enough for Converse and us to get along in. But I've been wrong."

"The whole world isn't big enough for Converse to get along with anybody but Converse, Buck. We found it so on the old Stony Ford range. We'll find it so in Gallatin. We might as well get this fact straight, once and for all. We've got to smash Luke Converse, or he'll smash us."

"We'll leave that to the future," said Custer thoughtfully. Buck Custer was a good fifteen years older than Dave Salkeld. He was a stocky, blunt-jawed man, beginning to grizzle about the ears. A peaceful man, Buck Custer, one who believed in live and let live. But if he had to, he could be a terror in a fight. He stirred restlessly. "How did you come out with DuBois, Dave?"

Salkeld's stern, fatigue-set lips quirked to a ghost of a smile. "I got our price out of him. He set out to jaw me down, but when I threatened to give the layout to Connors for nothing, he like to threw a fit and he nearly dislocated an arm getting his checkbook out. The money is in my saddlebags. Lord, I'm weary!"

Custer got back into the saddle. "I'll try and locate a sougan for you, kid. But I doubt my luck. The herd ran right over our camp. Devil only knows what's left of it."

It was good to sprawl there, right down on the clean, virile earth, to know that you had euchred one dirty ace that Luke Converse had dragged out of his deck. The cattle were no longer running, just moving at a weary, shuffling trot now. Soon they would stop. Soon the steady mutter of hoofs would die away, and then maybe he could sleep

Buck Custer came back a little later with the tattered remnants of a trampled sougan. Dave Salkeld was asleep and Custer threw a blanket over him. And left him there.

Under Custer's orders, the Flying Diamond riders did several things. They salvaged what they could of food and camp equipment and put it on pack horses. They let the herd rest an hour to quiet down. Then they slowly got it under way and headed it out of the swale and off to the south. Custer himself rode to the upper end of the swale and looked over the two crumpled figures he found lying there. "Mink Shroeder and Slim Laws," he muttered. "Dave is right. This is all the doings of Luke Converse. Well, if Converse wants to play the game this way, from now on he'll get as good as he sends."

CHAPTER TWO

The girl in the worn jeans and faded hickory shirt could not get over the wonder of it. She sat on the high seat of a staunch Conestoga wagon, looking out over the bedlam that was the Navajo River Meadows. Everywhere were wagons, everywhere were people, everywhere confusion, noise, and the restlessness of dammed-up human energy, fretting for release.

Maidie Abbott had never seen so many people in her life. From the height of her point of vantage she could look for miles, up and down the meadows. Yet, as far as the meadows stretched, there was nothing but this same crush of wagons, with humans to ride in them and horses to pull them. A human tide, beating at the barrier of time. At sunrise tomorrow this barrier would be lifted and the great land rush into the fabled Gallatin Basin would be on. She and her father and Lon Estes would be a part of that rush. The knowledge thrilled her to her fingertips. It was the great adventure of her life.

She was a slim, pretty girl in her early twenties, with a suntanned, wholesome face, merry of eye and mouth, with a powdering of freckles reaching across the bridge of her pert nose. For two long weeks she and her father had been on the trail, coming to this spot. They had left a comfortable, sedate little farm back in the Swamp River Valley. Maidie had been born and raised there. Yet, when her father had given way to the lure and dream of new land in a new wilderness and left the decision up to her, Maidie had not hesitated. She had been wild to go, from the first.

She had thought the Navajo River Meadows jammed with wagons and folks when she and her father arrived. But always were more and more wagons coming in, until the place was a swarming beehive. The same excitement that burned in her was in everyone else. You could sense it in the hoarse shouting of men, in the shrill, thin scolding of some tired woman. In the wail of a child, the shrill whistle of a restless horse.

Smoke of campfires rose everywhere. Cooking utensils clattered. Odors of cooking food lay on every slow turn of the air. Many hammers were at work, repairing, making ready. Axes were ringing on fuel for fires. In every sound lay that thread of excitement and tension. It was a buildup to the explosive beginning that would greet the rising sun on the following morning.

Maidie had a purpose besides just sitting on that wagon seat, looking around. Her father was off somewhere, making arrangements for freshly shoeing the team of solid work horses, a last vital item before the long trek started in the morning. And word had been passed about that thieves were in this crowd. Thieves and worse. So it behooved a guard to be about all wagons at all times. There was a rifle in the wagon, ready to Maidie's hand if she needed it.

It was inevitable that there be quantities of liquor in some of these wagons and Maidie had already seen several instances of drunkenness and brawling fights as a result of it. Far at the upper end of the meadows a troop of cavalry, assigned from Fort Ringgold, was in camp. These troops were to fire the official starting gun at sunrise on the morrow and during the interim were supposed to police the meadows until the tide was on its way. The soldiers were doing their best with the more belligerent of the settlers, but the meadows were large and there was much that escaped their notice.

It was a polyglot crowd that seethed and swirled and eddied

up and down the meadows. Most, of course, were gaunt, solid, raw-boned men in heavy boots and worn clothes. Men of the soil. Men like Maidie's father. But there were other types, also. Rough, swaggering adventurers. Good men, bad men, honest men, and thieves. Maidie saw several who her father had said were gamblers. There were men who walked alone, in whose narrowed eyes burned perpetual wariness and suspicion, men on the dodge. There was backbone and solid meat to this hegira, but there was riff-raff, too. And occasionally lean, brown men in spurs and chaps and broad hats, saddle men, drawn by the spice of adventure.

All these, as they passed, drew Maidie's eager eyes. They were integral parts of the picture, of its color and life. She didn't want to miss any part of that picture.

A mocking voice reached the girl's ears and abruptly she realized that she was the cause of what that voice was saying. She looked down from her point of vantage and saw four men in chaps and spurs and broad hats. One stood slightly in advance of the other three, feet spread, head and shoulders thrust forward in a sort of swaggering truculence. His face was slightly swarthy, bony, and hard, with a certain predatory handsomeness about it. There was a mocking boldness in his eyes that made Maidie stiffen and color slightly.

He laughed. "It is a girl, boys . . . and a darn' pretty one, too. I told you that shirt and those britches weren't fooling me any."

The other three laughed, too. "You always did have an eye for a pretty one, Luke," said one of them. "See can you get her to talk."

"Sure she'll talk," said the one called Luke. "I'm going to get right up there on that wagon and talk with her the rest of the afternoon. They always talk with me."

He swaggered forward, raised a booted foot to the hub of a front wheel of the wagon, and started to lift himself up. Maidie's hand shot back into the wagon, snapped her father's rifle into view, and jabbed the muzzle against the fellow's chest, hard—hard enough to knock the fellow backwards, where he sprawled on the earth. Whereupon his companions went into spasms of uncontrolled mirth, doubling over and beating their fists on their knees.

Maidie was scared. Her first swift moves had been purely instinctive. She hadn't meant to jab the fellow that hard. But now that the issue was up, she wasn't afraid to stand by her guns.

The man got up off the ground, no longer grinning mockingly. His face was twisted with a swift fury and there was a cruel, red spark burning in his eyes.

"So that's the game, eh?" he gritted. "Regular little hellcat, ain't you? We'll see about that."

He started forward again, but stopped abruptly as the gunlock *snicked* and Maidie brought the weapon to her shoulder. "Get back!" she ordered sharply. She was surprised how steady and firm her voice was. "Get back! You try to get on this wagon and I'll pull the trigger."

The fellow stopped. He didn't know whether she meant that threat, or not. But she might. That was just it—she might. At this range, she couldn't miss.

The others had stopped their hilarity. "Lay off, Luke," growled one of them. "You'll have us all in a jackpot in a minute. We'll have a flock of these sodbusters around our ears if you don't calm down. We ain't any too popular with 'em as it is. And if one of those damn' soldiers happens along . . . yeah, lay off."

The fellow shrugged. "All right," he mumbled. "But remember this, my smart young lady . . . I'll see you again. You're heading for Gallatin Basin. You wouldn't be here if you weren't. Well, I'll be in Gallatin Basin, too. And I'll see you again. Don't forget that. And the name, just so you'll remember, is Luke Converse."

Maidie said nothing. She just kept looking down the sights of the rifle, with one slim forefinger curled around the trigger. She didn't put the weapon down until Luke Converse and his companions had disappeared in the crush of wagons.

Then she was scared. She shook all over, and she uncocked the rifle and put it back in the wagon with a little shudder. She was thinking what would have happened had she really pressed the trigger. Suddenly some of the color and romance of this gathering faded and she sensed the cold ruthlessness of what a lawless frontier could be like.

A burly, bearded man came hurrying up, and, at sight of him, Maidie gave a little cry of relief and scrambled off the wagon box. "Dad!" she called breathlessly. "Dad!"

Jim Abbott looked at his daughter, startled by the tone of her voice. "What is it, lass?"

Maidie told him, and, although he scowled at first, he laughed and gave her a squeeze when she told him about knocking Converse off the wagon wheel with the rifle muzzle. "That's the girl," he said, applauding. "Don't you take a bit of fresh guff from any of these plug-uglies hanging around. You did just right. And don't you be a bit afraid to use that rifle on one of them, if he won't listen to any other sort of language. Now forget it. We got to get busy. My turn at the forge is coming up next. We got to get the horses over there right away, before somebody else beats me to it. Come on. The wagon will be all right."

The horses had been tied to the rear of the wagon and now they led them away, Abbott carrying a small toolbox besides. The forge lay nearer the river, and, when Maidie and her father got there, another settler had just finished using it.

Jim Abbott got to work industriously, bringing fresh horseshoes from his toolbox, tucking them into the coals, laying out his equipment for the job. Maidie worked the crudely constructed bellows and enjoyed hearing the whistling of the air and seeing the heart of the forge deepen to a white, glowing heat.

Over west, the sun was dropping very low. Jim Abbot worked fast. Dusk came swiftly in this country. Faintly in the distance the golden, stirring notes of a bugle lifted and fell, and Maidie knew that the flag at the cavalry camp was being lowered for the night. The sound of the bugle brought back to Maidie much of her thrilling anticipation of the adventure ahead. Somehow a bugle song hinted of frontiers, of movement and color.

For a second time she was jerked abruptly from her dreams. For a second time a harsh voice impinged upon her consciousness.

"All right, Abbott . . . your time is up. Camp rules are you can't keep that forge over half an hour. And you've had it longer than that now. Me and the boys got some tires to set and daylight will soon be gone."

The speaker was a lank, thin oldster, bearded and with ragged hair framing a narrow, sullen-looking face. Behind him stood four younger men, cut from the same lanky, hatchet-faced mould, and holding two heavy wagon tires between them.

Jim Abbott looked at them calmly. "You're wrong, Tremper," he rumbled. "I know of no such rule about this forge. I had to wait my turn." He turned to Maidie. "All right, lass . . . swing the bay around."

Maidie obeyed, backing one of the horses closer to the forge. Her father tonged a smoking shoe from the forge, lifted one of the bay's hoofs, and worked at the fitting, calm and unhurried as a bear.

Tremper stared at him, loose lips pealing back in anger. Then he whirled and rasped an order to his sons. They moved up, raked another shoe from the forge, and set one of the wagon

21

tires on the glowing coals.

"You're through hogging this forge, Abbott," snarled Tremper. "Me and my boys are taking over."

Jim Abbott straightened and a blaze came into his deep-set eyes. With a sweep of his arm he threw Tremper aside, grabbed the tire from the boys, and hurled it to the ground.

"Stand back!" he growled. "You fellows get this forge when I'm done with it, not before. If you had tended to business when you first hit this camp, instead of putting in all your time drinking and gambling and raising hell in general, you wouldn't be caught short like this. Get back! I'm in no mood to stand any foolishness from any of you."

He turned to pick up the shoe they had thrown from the forge, and, as he turned his back, as though by some unspoken signal, the five Trempers swarmed at him like a pack of wolves. Maidie, her heart in her throat, cried: "Dad! Look out!"

The advantage of the Trempers over brawny Jim Abbott was only temporary. He came up out of the crush, roaring mightily. His heavy fists began to smash and club and the snarling pack drew back. The affair took on an uglier look. Two of the Trempers drew knives. The rest caught up heavy billets of wood from beside the forge. They began to circle, watching their chance.

Maidie's first fear gave way to a flaming anger, which was mixed with fear for her father's safety. The sullen gleam of those bared knives made her queerly sick, but such was the state of her emotions, she overcame even this. Watching her chance, she darted forward and tried to wrest one of the knives from its owner. The fellow cursed, jerked away, and gave her a backhanded blow that knocked her flat. She crawled back to her feet, dizzy and half stunned, but was heedless of everything now but a flaming fury. She was about to move in again when her father yelled to her: "No! Stay out of this, lass. I can handle these whelps. No, Maidie . . . stay out of it!"

Usually her father's word was law to the girl. But this was different. She stumbled forward again, only to stop abruptly as a hand fell on her shoulder. A crisp, cool voice sounded in her ears.

"Your father is right, miss. Let me act for you."

Before Maidie could answer, a lean, brown figure in chaps and spurs and wide sombrero slid past her, grabbed one of the knife holders, spun him around, and knocked him flat with a slashing punch. Then he snapped a hand past his hip and it came away bearing the blue-black bulk of a heavy gun. His voice crackled.

"That'll be all, you *hombres!* Back away! I don't know all the whys and wherefores of this thing, but five against one is a little too strong for me to stomach. Back away!"

The Trempers stopped their circling and under the steady eye of that gun drew sullenly to one side. The one who had been knocked down got to unsteady feet and stood snarling.

"I want a good look at you, saddle pounder," he mumbled. "A good look . . . so I'll remember you."

The cowboy smiled thinly. "I refuse to scare, you knife-handling coyote. So look away. And if it will help you, the name is Dave Salkeld. Now . . . git!"

The Trempers gathered up their wagon tires and slinked off. The cowboy turned away and was gathering up the reins of his horse when Jim Abbott came striding over to him, hand outstretched. "I'm Jim Abbott," he said heartily. "And I'm saying thanks, cowboy. It might have turned a little nasty if you hadn't stepped in. Maidie, lass . . . did that brute hurt you when he knocked you down?"

Maidie crept inside the circle of her father's arm. She laughed shakily. "My dignity, more than anything else, Dad. But when I saw those knives . . . I . . . I just saw red, too."

The strange cowboy nodded, smiling. "I saw that. It was a

spunky thing to do. Decided me, more than anything else, that it was time for me to take a hand. You heard me tell that whelp my name? Dave Salkeld?"

Maidie nodded, suddenly shy.

Her father spoke: "My daughter Maidie, Salkeld."

The cowboy's smile widened, to show even white teeth. "We meet under rather stormy circumstances. But I'm glad we've met, just the same. Now, Mister Abbott, you better get back at your job. Daylight is 'most gone."

"Right," said Abbott heartily. "I'm nearly done. Maidie, you better run along to the wagon and get supper started. I can finish alone. Hope to see you again, Salkeld."

Maidie headed for the wagon and found the cowboy walking beside her, leading his dusty, sweaty, weary horse. After her trouble with Luke Converse, Maidie wasn't feeling any too cordial toward cowboys. But this fellow was distinctly a different type than Converse. He was tall and lean, with a wide sweep of shoulder. But there was nothing swaggering about him. He prowled along beside her, easy and sure in his movements. His face was brown and hard and clean-cut, with a strong, clean jaw line. In the gleam of his eye and smile there was a spirit of daring, of adventure.

"These meadows," he said casually. "I can't get over them as they are now. A month ago I came through here. Then they were as empty and virgin as a dawn sky. Now look at 'em. A regular madhouse. I never knew there was this many people in the world."

Some of Maidie's shyness left her. She laughed. "I've had the same thought. They remind me of a swarm of bees, crawling all over everything, sizzling and humming."

"And tomorrow is the big day, eh?" he drawled.

"Tomorrow!" Maidie spoke the word breathlessly. "I can hardly wait. I bet I'll hardly sleep a wink tonight."

Salkeld chuckled. "That will be true of most of the camp, I suspect. Funny thing, this land hunger. Drives people loco. I'll bet a lot of people in this rush left perfectly good ranches and homes to gamble on a new country."

"I'm sure of it," admitted Maidie frankly. "I know Dad and I did. And I'm glad, no matter what we find in Gallatin Basin."

"I suppose your father has some idea of where he is going to settle?"

"Oh, yes. The Cache Creek country, wherever that is. A . . . a wild horse hunter is going to help Dad locate the place."

"Cache Creek!" exclaimed Salkeld. "Say, that's fine. I expect to be somewhere around there myself. Maybe we'll be neighbors."

Maidie flashed him a quick glance. "Maybe that would be bad. Cattlemen and settlers don't, as a rule, get along very well."

"Why not? I believe in living and let live."

"Then you are different from most cattlemen I've run across," retorted Maidie swiftly. "Well, here is the wagon. And . . . and I do thank you for all you did for Dad and me, Mister Salkeld."

Salkeld smiled that flashing smile again. "Lady, it was a pleasure. *Hasta luego.* Until we meet again." He touched his hat and went on, a lithe, smooth-moving figure, spurs *clanking* softly on the grass-blanketed meadow earth.

CHAPTER THREE

The farther Dave Salkeld moved along the river meadows, the denser became the crush of wagons. Wagons of all sorts. Prairie schooners, ponderous freight wagons, buckboards, spring wagons, buggies, carts. People and more people. Campfires. Dogs slinking about, fearful and quarrelsome. On the tail gate of one wagon was tied a coop of chickens, *squawking* forlornly. A gaunt, scared-looking cow, eyes wild and rolling, was snubbed close up against the rear of another wagon. There was one thing in common with all the larger wagons. Along the reach pole, underneath the wagon beds, was lashed a plow. The real symbol of an advancing civilization. The plow.

Through the ceaseless clamor of voices and excited activity, Dave caught the rippling tempo of an expertly strummed banjo and the mellow boom of a Negro voice. He headed that way and under a towering cottonwood tree found several cowboys grouped about a campfire. In the middle of the group sat the Negro singer, black face shining in the firelight glow.

At sight of Dave, the song broke off and the cowboys came crowding about. "Dog-gone your hide, Dave . . . you had us worried," growled Jumbo Curtis, a gigantic, immensely strong rider. "You shore cut the time pretty fine."

"Couldn't be helped," defended Dave. "One thing and another held me back. Mose, you black rascal, how about some grub? I'm wolfish."

The Negro scuttled away to a nearby trail wagon. "Right

away, Marse Dave . . . right away. Jest yo' sit yo'self down and old Mose'll have them victuals ready, *pronto.*"

Dave relaxed on the earth with a sigh of weariness. Tonto Rice, grizzled, leathery, thin-faced, cleared his throat and spat. "What held you back, kid? Old DuBois get stubborn on you?"

Dave shook his head. "DuBois came through all right. It was something else." And then Dave told the story of the stampede. When he finished, a mutter of anger ran through the group.

"That's Converse for you," rumbled Jumbo Curtis. "He's a dog. Mink Shroeder and Slim Laws, eh? Tried to stampede our herd right over Buck Custer and the other boys. And you got 'em both. That's good news. Maybe Buck Custer will realize now that there is only one way to handle Luke Converse . . . with a club."

"He realizes it," said Dave. "Buck is mad this time . . . plenty. Seen anything of Converse?"

"Have we! Sa-ay, him and Slim Jepson, Bob Chehallis, and Saugus Lee have been swaggering up and down these meadows, high and mighty as hell, picking an argument with some wagon man every fifteen feet. If somebody don't put a stop to it, we're going to find ourselves hated so bad in Gallatin Basin, we never will be able to get along with the wagon folks. Because they class all cattlemen in the same coop. Converse has got his C Cross herd massed over under Table Mountain. Tonto and me took a little ride this afternoon and looked things over. We figure Converse is set to jump the gun. He's got a few cattle across the river right now."

"He would," said Dave. "Always wanting the edge, that juniper. But he's got his troubles ahead. You can move cattle just so fast. Time he gets his herd to Gallatin, he'll find most of the water settled on and nowhere to light. Our plan is better. We go in fast, at the head of the rush, stake our claims and file them, then bring in our cattle later. That way we're sure of range to put them on. Where you got our horses?"

"Back under the rim in a thicket of aspen. Pudge is guarding them now," said Jumbo. "You das'n't leave a thing unguarded around here, Dave. There are plenty of good, honest folks in this mob, but there are a lot of no-good mavericks, too. Good thing the jump-off is tomorrow morning, else everything would end up in one big brawl. The excitement and tension have got a lot of these people half loco."

Mose brought a plate of steaming food and Dave ate hungrily. "Mose," he said, "don't you let the excitement get the best of you and turn you reckless with that wagon. You take your time. We're going to need the grub and supplies you're hauling. If you break down along the trail and leave us flat . . . well, you better start running."

Mose showed all his teeth in a huge grin. "Don't you worry none about old Mose, Marse Dave. I'se gonna be plumb keerful."

Darkness lay over the world in a velvet blanket. Some of the confused clamor along the meadows faded out. People were thinking of what the morrow might bring to them. After all, this was going to be a jump-off into the unknown. And no man could weigh the chances of the unknown, whether it held happiness or sorrow, life or death. The older, more sober minds were realizing this.

Mose brought his banjo to the fire again and his voice lifted once more in song. The music brought spectators and listeners. The group about the cowboys' fire thickened. Gaunt, bearded men. Tired, stooped women, the vague light of dreams still in their patient eyes. And a few of the older children, awed to silence by the soberness of their elders. Under the stimulus of this audience, Mose spread himself. Rollicking tunes where Mose's voice seemed to laugh set boots to tapping in time. And then sad, plaintive tunes, old folk songs and spirituals in which

Mose lost himself in all his native heritage of lonely melancholy. At these times men would stare broodingly into the flames, while the women would touch furtive fingers to their eyes.

There was a rustle of movement beside Dave Salkeld and he looked up to behold Jim Abbott and his daughter. Dave smiled a welcome and made room for them. Maidie had changed to a simple dress of gingham and Dave was struck anew by her prettiness and wholesome charm.

"Who is he?" she asked softly, nodding at Mose.

Dave chuckled. "That's Mose, our cook."

"He's priceless," said Maidie. "That music . . . some of it makes me want to laugh. And then again I want to cry."

"He's pretty good at this music business, for a fact. And a swell cook. He'll do to take along, any old time, Mose will. Get those bronc's shod, Mister Abbott?"

"Oh, yes. Incidentally, Salkeld, I'm afraid you've made yourself some enemies, stepping in to help Maidie and me the way you did. That Tremper crowd are a poisonous lot, and good haters. Keep an eye on them."

Dave shrugged. "Just a flock of coyotes, yelping in the dark. Thanks for warning me, though."

Sly old Mose, seeing his beloved boss sitting in conversation with a distinctly pretty girl, went into an old-time love song, and with an impudence amounting almost to genius left little doubt as to where his words were aimed.

Soft color washed Maidie's throat and cheeks and she stared at the ground with confused eyes as a chuckle ran through the listening crowd. Jim Abbott rumbled with mirth. "Face it out, lass," he murmured. "That black rascal is only funnin' you."

"Mose," called Dave, "I'll give you a taste of my quirt if you don't stop teasing the lady!"

Mose let out a great shout of laughter. "Marse Dave, I cut off my right hand before I make that li'l missy feel bad. Come on, folks, everybody dance."

Black fingers twinkled and the music took on an irresistible tempo. A young wagon man caught his wife about the waist and began whirling her about. Immediately there were others, until a full dozen couples were dancing. Mose whooped, swung into a Virginia reel, shouting off the changes.

A shy, awkward youngster, still lacking two or three years of his majority, touched Maidie Abbott on the shoulder. She looked up into his honest eyes, nodded, and jumped to her feet. And the two of them joined the dancers.

Jim Abbott leaned toward Dave. "This is good stuff," he said. "Take people's minds off what tomorrow may hold for them."

The dance went on with the older folks, who did not dance, clapping their hands and stamping their feet in cadence. And then came a harsh interruption. There was a stir of confusion among the dancers, and a sharp protest in a feminine voice. Dave Salkeld jerked to his feet and a harsh exclamation broke from his lips.

Maidie Abbott and her youthful partner were struggling with a swaggering, arrogant man in cowboy clothes. It was Luke Converse. And he was holding Maidie with one hand while he pushed her partner away with the other. His voice was heavy and mocking. "The lady yearns to dance with a man, not a half-weaned pup. Get back, before I slap you down."

Maidie's youthful partner did not lack for spunk. He aimed a futile blow at Converse, who laughed cruelly and knocked the lad flat with a savage punch.

A rising growl of anger went through the wagon folks, but it was Dave Salkeld who acted. Beyond Converse he saw the shadowy figures of a couple of the brutal cattleman's riders.

"Jumbo . . . Tonto," rasped Dave. "Back my hand. Keep an eye on the other coyotes."

Then Dave went through the crowd with a rush, breaking

This was a cue for Mose. "Come on, folks!" he shouted. "Eve'ybody sing!"

Mose swung into the stirring, marching lilt of "Oh, Susanna." Somehow it seemed that this was exactly what the crowd had been waiting for. Here was a tune to lift up their hearts, banish all doubt and fear of the morrow. It stirred their blood as it had that of countless pioneers before them. It was the song men had sung while taming a great continent. With Mose's mellow voice to lead them, while the banjo strummed madly, they did sing.

The voices of men, harsh and untrained. Those of women, thin and plaintive. They sang it with upturned faces and shining eyes. In it there was a melody, a spirit, a sturdiness and courage unquenchable. For this night would soon be done. And on the morrow they would be marching . . . marching. . . .

clearly beside Maidie and Converse. He blasted a thunderous punch under Luke Converse's ear, knocking him down. Dave caught Maidie by the arm. "Back to your Dad," he said harshly. "This hawg needs a lesson."

Jumbo Curtis and Tonto Rice faced Bob Chehallis and Saugus Lee with drawn guns. "Back away," rapped Tonto thinly. "Converse travels this trail alone, and it's going to be a rocky one."

Converse was still on the ground, muddled and dazed. Dave Salkeld leaned over him, jerked his guns away, and tossed them aside. He unbuckled his own gun belts and handed them to one of the wagon men. He jabbed Converse to his feet with a boot toe.

"All right, Converse," he gritted. "You got a licking coming. You get it now."

Converse glared at him, lowered his head, and charged in. He was heavier than Dave, with a savage, raw-boned power about him, and he distinctly fancied himself as a rough-and-tumble fighter. But he ran into an uppercut that straightened him and brought a smear of blood from his snarling lips. Then came a hooking right fist that spun him half around.

Converse roared like a wounded grizzly and leaped at Dave, to be met with a straight, lashing fist that made a mess of his mouth and loosened half a dozen teeth. As Converse tottered on his heels, Dave moved in and knocked him down with another right hook to the jaw.

The first surprised tension left the crowd. Wagon men thrust wives and daughters back and crowded into a tense, savage circle about the fighters. Shouts of encouragement for Dave rose. "Go get him, cowboy! Knock his brains out! Put the boots to him!"

Dave let Converse get up. There was a dark, glowering surprise in Converse's moiling eyes. He wasn't used to being knocked down in a fist fight by a lighter man than himself. He crouched, pulled his numbed jaw well down against his chest, and moved in slowly, hands reaching and clawing.

Mose, standing on tiptoe by the fire, yelled excitedly: "Don't let him git hold of you, Marse Dave! He aims to use you foul, kin he do so. Watch him, Marse Dave . . . watch him!"

Converse came in with a crouched, squatting rush. Dave side-stepped, aiming a punch. But the crowding circle had narrowed too much. Dave collided with a wagon man, missed his punch. And then Converse closed with him, snarling with triumph.

Converse jerked Dave to him, his heavy, raw-boned arms encircling Dave and setting tightly in a bear hug. "Now, damn you," panted Converse, "we'll see . . . we'll see!"

The man, driven by fury, was terrifically strong. To Dave Salkeld it felt as though a steel band was crushing out his life. His breath left him with a gasp of agony. He could feel his ribs spring, his spine being slowly but surely cracked. His ears filled with sodden roaring and crazy lights flashed before his eyes. In another moment he was sure his back would be broken. There was only one thing for Dave to do, and he did it.

He gave way suddenly, throwing himself backward. His shoulders and head struck the ground with wicked impact, half stunning him. But Converse, heavy body thrown up and forward by Dave's sudden effort, took it worse. His face drove past Dave's shoulder and smashed hard against the ground and his neck was nearly dislocated as his body swung over and down. His hold on Dave was broken, and Dave got to stumbling, faltering feet, gulping air into his tortured lungs.

Converse came up very slowly, spitting and snarling. His face was black and swollen, his lips split and puffed, blood running from mouth and nose. His hands reached out again, trying once more to get hold of Dave.

But Dave kept away from him, waiting for the sweet night air to bring back precious vigor and vitality. When strength lay strong in him again, he still faked weakness and desperation. Converse, fooled by the play, leaped at him, wide open, while his hands reached and clawed.

Dave straightened like a released spring. He started the punch clear from his heels, and the power of it surged all through his forward-driving body. Everything he had went into that punch, and it caught Converse fully in the face with a sodden, sledge-hammer impact. Dave had never hit a man as he hit Converse that time.

Converse stopped as though he had run into a battering ram. He trembled all over, like a tree shaken to the heart by a woodsman's axe. His arms fell weakly to his sides. His head rolled around and around in a loose circle. A deep, mortal groan retched from his pulped lips. Then he fell forward on his face, and lay there, twitching and helpless.

Dave stepped back, breathing deeply. "Tonto, Jumbo!" he called harshly. "Bring those other two coyotes here to pack him away. We don't want him lying around our camp."

Under the guns of Tonto and Jumbo, Saugus Lee and Bob Chehallis came, black-browed and scowling. They hoisted Converse to his feet and took him away, Converse's feet dragging and stumbling.

Dave pushed through the crowd to the fire, where Mose was almost whimpering with joy. A bear trap grip shook his right hand. It was Jim Abbott. "A clean job, well done," said Abbott, his voice deep with emotion. "You made a bitter enemy this night, Dave Salkeld. But you made more friends."

Maidie Abbott was there, too. She looked up at Dave in wordless awe, her eyes enormous pools of shadow in her pale face. Dave grinned at her. "Too bad the dance had to be broken up," he said.

CHAPTER FOUR

Gray dawn seeped over the world. Along the river ghostly mists weaved and coiled. At the distant cavalry camp a bugle sounded the notes of "Reveille." A stir of activity spread swiftly. Morning fires began to *crackle* and gleam. Women cooked breakfast while men led horses to the river to drink. Now that the deadline was fast approaching, there were many who found a number of things still undone. The stir of activity took on a certain confusion.

The friendliness of the night was gone. Now men eyed each other suspiciously, truculently, beginning to edge their wagons a little more into the clear, jockeying for starting positions. In this maneuvering, two wagons locked wheels. Neither driver would give way, and, after a short, fierce argument, they leaped to the ground and began swinging heavy blows at each other.

Cavalry men, moving out to take posts along the river to see that no too-eager settler jumped the gun, parted the two fighters, calming them with curt, harsh words.

A little farther along, a wagon had backed over a Dutch oven belonging to a neighboring camp. The ensuing brawl had two men in a wild tangle on the ground. Again a cavalryman intervened. The atmosphere along the meadows was becoming explosive.

Dave Salkeld and his companions were up early, breakfast eaten and all equipment stowed securely in Mose's wagon. Horses were brought in and saddled. And then Dave, with sunup still some distance away, wandered off through the tangle.

A great day, this. He, along with all these other folks, had planned and worked and sweated toward this day. Like him, they were gambling on the future—a future where some would win and others inevitably lose. That was life.

Dave smiled a trifle grimly as he realized where his steps were leading him. Well, why not? Twice had fate thrown him into the breach when trouble had threatened Jim Abbott and his daughter. Dave had the feeling that he had known both of them a long time. And Maidie—well, Dave had never known a girl quite like her. There was so much about her that was strong and eager and wholesome.

He found them about ready for the start. Maidie, again in overalls and faded shirt, was loading the last of the cooking utensils into the wagon. Jim Abbott had his team already hitched and was going around the wagon, making sure that everything was secure.

Maidie met Dave's grin with a gay smile. "Jump-off day," said Dave. "I bet you're about ready to pop."

Her laugh was breathless. "Rather about ready to fly. Was anything ever so slow as that sun!"

There was a lithe, soft-footed man in chaps and spurs who was helping Jim Abbott about the wagon. Jim Abbott made the introduction. "Shake hands with Lon Estes, Salkeld."

Lon Estes's hand was wiry and supple. His face was thin and hard. His eyes were brown, almost to blackness. He carried two big guns, slung low and tied down. His nod was curt and he did not speak, his lips thin and tight.

Dave's mental cataloguing said: *Gunfighter, and a tough one.* Aloud, Dave said: "Hope you got your water keg good and full, Mister Abbott. The country between here and Gallatin Basin is a pretty dry stretch."

Abbott pounded his thigh with a clenched fist. "Dog-gone! I

had forgotten that water keg."

"Break it out and I'll help you fill it," said Dave.

Lon Estes spoke for the first time, his voice tight and dry and colorless. "No need, Salkeld. Jim and me can handle that."

Jim Abbott, looking a little uncomfortable, got the water keg, and he and Estes headed for the river with it. Maidie turned to Dave soberly, her eyes searching his face. "First it was at the forge . . . then it was at the dance last night," she said gravely. "Each time you stepped in to save Dad or me some unpleasantness and trouble. You've been good to us, Dave Salkeld. Why?"

It was a fair question and he gave her a fair answer. "Because I like your father and I like you."

For a moment their eyes held. Then color washed warmly up her slender throat and her eyes fell. Her laugh was soft, uncertain. "That seems to be a pretty good reason, Dave Salkeld. So . . . until we meet again . . . good trailing." She held out her hand and he took it, pressing it warmly.

"That's right," said Dave. "*Hasta luego* . . . and good trailing. And I'll be seeing you, somewhere along Cache Creek."

Dave moved off through the tangle of activity. All about him men were on wagon boxes, reins in hand, booted feet on brakes, ready to kick free and drive at a second's notice. Women in calico and sunbonnets were perched beside their men, and tousled heads of children peered from the wagon. Time was growing short.

Here and there, men who had been present at the fight the night before hailed Dave with friendly nods. Dave answered with a grin and wave.

Then something *hissed* past Dave's throat, a *hiss* ending in a solid, heavy *tunk*. Dave's eyes saw a startling thing. There, sticking in the hard, seasoned wood of a wagon side right before him was a heavy knife, still quivering with the force of the throw.

Dave whirled to see a lank figure dodging off through the

wagons. Dave went after him, dragging a gun, and caught up with the fugitive just as the fellow tried to scramble over the tailgate of a rickety prairie schooner. It was one of the narrow-faced, venomous Tremper boys. Dave, simmering with fury over the cowardly attempt to knife him, gun-whipped the recreant solidly, dropping him in a heap.

There was a blast of savage cursing from the wagon and a rifle barrel licked out over the tailgate. Dave grabbed the threatening muzzle with his left hand and pushed it aside. And he shoved his gun right up against the face of old Zeph Tremper.

"Don't try it," rasped Dave. "Else I'll spatter what few brains you have all over this wagon. Call your worthless litter off. I don't handle 'em easy any more. The next one who makes a pass at me, gets it. Savvy?"

A driver from a neighboring wagon, who had seen it all, whooped encouragement. "Go ahead, cowboy! Blow his topknot off. Ain't an ounce of decent color in the whole damned Tremper crew. Let him have it!"

As Zeph Tremper loosened his grip on the rifle, Dave jerked it from him and threw it under the wagon. At that moment a long, shrill yell echoed all up and down the meadows.

"Get your spurs set, you land hunters! They're rolling the starting gun into position. Let 'em buck!"

Dave backed away from the Tremper wagon, then hurried for his own camp. Everything was in readiness. There were three horses for each man, to be ridden in relays. That way, they could cover a maximum of space in a minimum of time. For, after all, this whole thing was a race. The law would recognize the ownership of the first to make and file his claim.

Dave looked over his crew. Tonto Rice, grizzled and leathery. Jumbo Curtis, big and hulking, with a booming voice and garrulous tongue, but all man, just the same. And there was Pudge

Herkimer and Wampus Collins and Dirk Bender. Tried and true, these men, who would back Dave's hand to the edge of hell and beyond, if it were necessary. Wampus and Dirk, the youngest, were fairly squirming in their saddles with impatience.

Dave threw an expert glance at the eastern horizon. It was all rose and gold now. The sun was due.

Along the meadows, men with set, strained faces were leaning forward on their wagon seats as though the very tenseness of their hunched bodies would help lift the heavy Conestogas into movement.

There was a moment of comparative silence, then, as the rim of the world away out in the rose and gold east grew brighter and brighter, a murmur swept over the meadows, growing louder and louder until it was a shrill, penetrating din.

Came a wild yell. "The sun! There's the sun! There . . . !"

BOOM!

Down at the cavalry camp a small field piece belched a huge cloud of smoke, bucked in recoil, and sent the wild echoes rolling. It was the jump-off!

The echoes of the cannon shot were drowned in a mad wave of human clamor. Whips snapped like pistol shots and the first wave of wagons struck the river in a landslide of confusion and noise.

Dave and his men hit the water at a sane pace, giving their horses a chance. But just below them a settler, mad with excitement, lashed his team into a frenzied leap off a sheer, four-foot bank. The wagon, careening after the frantic animals, dropped heavy front wheels over the bank, struck hard, and turned completely over, throwing the driver headlong into the river.

Just above, two wagons fighting for the same narrow ford, locked wheels and came to a grinding stop. A third wagon smashed into them, complicating the tangle in the boiling river waters. Men bawled furiously, cursing and raving. A woman screamed in fright. A dog, flipped from a jouncing wagon, came up in a boiling flurry, swam to the far bank, and raced yelping away, terrified half out of its senses by the mad confusion. Somewhere along the river a gunshot sounded, then two more in quick and deadly reply.

Near at hand another gun rapped, and something struck the horn of Dave Salkeld's saddle with a shock that left him tingling all over. Almost stupidly he stared down at the lead-torn rawhide covering of his steel-cored saddle horn. Then he realized that the bullet had not been merely a stray one. His head jerked up. A little below him a vaguely familiar wagon was lurching and reeling over the hidden boulders of the river bottom. One of the hatchet-faced Trempers was driving it and Dave was just in time to see a rifle barrel being withdrawn behind a flap of the canvas cover.

Cold fury whipped through Dave. All in one move he dragged a gun and smashed a shot at the spot where that rifle barrel disappeared. He heard a howl of agony. He would have shot again except that another wagon came lunging along to block out the Tremper layout.

Still simmering with anger, Dave felt his pony strike the far shelving bank and scramble up it, his relay broncos scrambling behind. The rest of his boys were safely over and Dave holstered his gun. He'd be seeing that Tremper crowd again, over in Gallatin.

The first of the wagons had made the crossing safely. Once clear of the crush, many of the wagon men showed their good judgment by setting their horses to a steady, reasonable pace, realizing that Gallatin Basin was still a long way off and that the surest way to thwart their own purpose was to run their teams to death in the first mile or two.

But there were others, still crazy with excitement, who flogged their teams to a run, the heavy wagons bouncing and clattering.

One of these, drawing out ahead of the rest, could not resist standing on his wagon box, turning and yelling exultant taunts at those more sober ones behind. While he was doing this, his foaming team ran right off into a deep, narrow dry wash that the river at some past flood time had cut apart from its regular channel. Horses and wagon came down into the dry wash with a wild crash. The wagon tongue snapped, a front wheel dished, and the whole thing turned over. The taunter, flung headlong against the far bank of the wash, lay crumpled just where he landed, his head twisted at a sharp and sickening angle.

Tonto Rice spurred up beside Dave. "Crazy," he yelled. "All of them. Crazy as locoed cattle. Tomorrow a man can trace the trail to Gallatin Basin by the broken wagons along the way."

Dave nodded, murmuring to himself: "Broken wagons, and broken hearts, too."

Already the high hopes and dreams of many of the settlers had been crushed. More of the same would come, for the trail to Gallatin was long and rough. Dave wondered about the Abbotts. He hoped Jim Abbott had kept his head, that he had fought off the virus of crazy excitement that had led to the early downfall of so many other settlers. Maidie Abbott—she would be on the wagon seat beside her father, her eyes shining and dreamy with the adventure that lay beyond the rolling hills. Dave wished them a silent and fervent good luck.

By this time, the mounts of Dave and his men had settled to a steady, ground-eating pace. They moved out ahead of all the wagons. Other saddle men began moving after them, spurring fast to come even and then go out ahead. But Dave let them go, setting his own pace and holding it. For a long race was won at the finish, not at the start.

CHAPTER FIVE

Once clear of the uncertain terrain of the river bottoms, and into the rolling hills beyond, which billowed up to a low crest, the multitudinous units of the land rush spread swiftly. Topping that crest, Dave Salkeld turned in his saddle and looked back. Wagons to his left, wagons to his right, almost as far as the eye could reach, the distant ones looking like a swarm of ungainly beetles, creeping along over the wide distances.

A bearded ancient on an old, bony white mule came *clattering* along, meager pack bounding wildly behind his rugged saddle. He was quirting the mule at every jump and the animal was already showing signs of exhaustion. Dave reined over beside the old fellow.

"What's the big rush, old-timer?" he yelled jocularly. "Want to kill that mule off? You'll be afoot in another ten minutes if you don't slack up."

The old fellow blinked at Dave a little stupidly, as though just awakening from some wild nightmare. For the first time he seemed to realize the condition of his aged mount. He threw his quirt away and pulled up. Watching over his shoulder, Dave saw the old fellow dismount and put his arms about the mule's sagging head. And when, half a mile farther on, Dave looked back again, he saw the tiny white object that was the mule, with a tinier figure trudging sturdily along beside the animal. Dave chuckled, shaking his head. You couldn't figure the human animal when the free land madness was upon him. His vagaries

42

of mind were too confusing.

Looking ahead, Dave saw, far out to the southwest, dim and hazy in the morning mists, a long, low, flat-topped line against the horizon. Although this line showed a blackish purple at the base, the crest of it was beginning to burn a deep, rich vermilion. This line of color was the Vermilion Wall. Somewhere near the center of that wall, as yet hidden by the extreme distance, was a narrow cut, the gateway to that promised land, Gallatin Basin.

Tonto Rice spurred up beside Dave and, without a word, pointed to the northeast. Out there, under the rising ball of the sun, lay the black bulk of a tableland. Along the foot of that tableland a faint plume of dust glinted, gray-brown in the sharp sunlight.

"Cattle," said Dave. "Converse is on the drive with his herd."

"Right," said Tonto. "Navajo River curves 'way to the north of Table Mountain. That dust is a good ten miles past the river now. Which means that Converse did jump the gun. He shoved that herd across the river some time last night."

Beyond the rolling hills lay sagebrush country, sweeping out and out like a gray mist, to wash finally against the distant Vermilion Wall. The climbing sun had already sucked up the coolness of the vanished night, and now its heat, in increasing waves, began to roll across the world.

As yet no wagon had topped the crest of the rolling hills and entered the sage country. Only saddle men, like himself, were in Dave's view, some ahead, some behind, some even. There was one on a smoothly running sorrel who crept up, held even, and then moved ahead. Dave recognized Lon Estes, the gunman friend of the Abbotts. Estes looked neither to right or left, his face a thin, hard mask under the shadow of his sweeping sombrero brim.

When Dave figured he had put a good ten miles behind him, he reined in and switched his saddle to one of his relay broncos, his companions doing the same. Then it was once more the settled, measured stride of running hoofs, the gray sage sweeping by endlessly on either hand, and out ahead, burning with a more deeply savage color all the time, Vermilion Wall, seemingly just as far away as ever, as though mocking the puny efforts of men and horses.

Far back, the first wagons had topped the rolling hills and were now tiny, lurching bulks against the vast spread of sage country. Another ripple of that tide of empire that had claimed a continent. Ponderous, slow, but indomitably sure.

Dave and his men rode stoically, making saddle changes at regular intervals. Now the value of this strategy became apparent. They began overhauling and passing riders on single mounts, who had spurred so recklessly ahead, running those broncos not wisely but too hard. Some of these riders waved in good-natured resignation as Dave and his men swept by. Others cursed and shook their fists. They passed one man whose horse had dropped and died. The fellow was sitting on the dead animal, shoulders hunched, head sunk in his hands, either from remorse or despair, Dave could not tell which.

Mid-afternoon came and passed. The Vermilion Wall rose higher and higher before them, hot and glowing and weirdly red, terrifying in its barren, scorched loneliness, in those deep, ferocious colors. The trapped heat of the day struck them in a thickening wave as they moved into the first reaches of the defile that cut through the great wall. They were tiny atoms of living matter, dwarfed almost to nothingness under the solid, elemental power of the wall.

"Antelope Pass," mumbled Dave through dust-crusted, heat-parched lips, pointing to the defile ahead. "It'll be hot in there."

It was. Dave made another saddle change. All of the horses were gaunt and weary now, scabby with dried sweat. The men gulped, open-mouthed, at the furnace air. At the foot of the west wall of the pass, shadows were beginning to form, deep purple and as thick as turgid oil. But there was no coolness in those shadows.

On and on, with the rimrocks of the pass seeming to press in like savage jaws about to close and crush forever the puny humans riding beneath them. The floor of the pass was sand, strangely orange in color, smeared here and there by stunted, tenacious sage.

They crept past the base of a huge battlement of sandstone that speared the sunset sky in a terrific blaze of color. There they came upon another dead horse, a sorrel, with a lithe, hard-faced rider kneeling beside the saddle he had just stripped from the luckless animal. The man was Lon Estes.

Dave reined in beside him. "It's been in my mind, ever since you passed us, that you might be aiming to line up a good piece of ground for Jim Abbott," said Dave, his voice dry and thick. "Is that right?"

Lon Estes stared back at him with those brownish-black, unreadable eyes. "And if I am?" he said, his voice toneless.

"Then I'll loan you a bronc'. They're none too stout right now, but with careful riding they'll get you through. How about it?"

The gunman hesitated, then nodded. "You guessed right," he said.

He saddled one of Dave's relay and dropped in beside Dave, riding silently.

It seemed, shortly after, that they passed a sort of crest, there in the heart of the pass. From there led a downward slope with the horses moving with less effort. Sunset was at hand. The whole pass was swimming with color, still bright crimson along the rimrocks, deepening to rich purple in the depths, with the gut of the pass filling with what seemed powder-blue smoke.

A breath of cooler air struck their faces. They sucked it up avidly, men and horses alike. That current of air grew stronger with each passing moment until it became a breeze, then a rushing wind, and the contrast to the past hours of deadening heat made it seem almost cold. In it, too, there was the scent of moisture and the breath of far-off timbered slopes.

Dave turned to Tonto Rice, his voice lifting to a shout above the rising wind. "Gallatin Basin just ahead. From now until about midnight it will be a hurricane blowing through the pass. Buck Custer and I got caught in it when we came through a month ago. It like to blew us apart."

At last they were out of the pass and ahead of and below them lay a vast gulf of country, swimming in twilight mists. The slope steepened and soon they were into breast-high sagebrush, then into scrub pine, and finally into towering timber and cool, dark depths where living water ran.

Dave reined in and dismounted. "We camp here," he croaked. "Watch your bronc's. Don't let them founder themselves on that water."

They fought the frantic animals back from the creek, letting the thirsty brutes drink but a little at first, then fully slake ravening thirst a little later. Men drank and bathed dusty, sun-scorched faces. They built a small fire and made a frugal scanty meal from the supplies carried behind their saddles. While the weary horses foraged on the tender browse along the creek, men flattened out beside the fire.

"Me," said Jumbo Curtis, "I hate to think of the job it is going to be, bringing our herd through that stretch of country. We're going to lose cows, Dave."

"Some," admitted Dave. "Not too many if we use our heads. We'll rest and water the herd well at Navajo River. We'll pull out from there about mid-afternoon and drive straight through. That will give us the advantage of one whole night of cool travel that will get the herd over most of the country the other side

Vermilion Wall in good shape. The next day will be a tough one, all right. But we'll keep 'em moving and get them through Antelope Pass by sundown of the next day. This water will be here waiting for the herd. Buck and me figured the whole thing out. We're going to lose some cows, all right, but that kind of a drive can be done."

"That wind blowing through the pass shore is a queer thing," said Pudge Herkimer. "Listen to it, will you? Makes a man's spine sort of creep."

The others could hear it easily enough. A far-off, shrill, wailing moan, eerie in the blackness.

"Creepy is right," said Wampus Collins, the kid of the outfit.

Lon Estes took no part in the conversation. He lounged on one elbow, staring at the shortening flames of the fire with narrowed, inscrutable eyes. In the firelight his face looked almost brittle, so thin and sharp was it.

Whatever Dave Salkeld's riders thought of his generosity in loaning this strange rider a horse, they kept it to themselves. All of them could read Estes for the sort of man he was. He had all the earmarks. A lone wolf of a gunman, shrouded in his own thoughts.

Dave tossed his cigarette butt into the coals. "Turn in," he ordered. "We got another long day ahead."

"Wonder how Mose is making it," said Jumbo, trying to find a soft place for his head on his saddle.

"Don't you worry none about Mose," answered Tonto Rice. "He's got a full water keg, a sound team of horses, and a stout wagon. He'll let the other wagons beat a trail for him through the rough places. A mighty shrewd old darky, Mose is."

Just before he fell asleep, Dave Salkeld wondered about another wagon and the glowing-eyed girl who would be riding on it.

CHAPTER SIX

When the echoes of the starting cannon rumbled over the Navajo River Meadows, it seemed to Maidie Abbott that something wild and surging had been let loose within her. Had she been handling the reins, she would have sent horses and wagon hurtling madly ahead in a reckless endeavor to be first across the river. But Jim Abbott owned a sage, cool head. With almost maddening deliberation, he kicked off the brake, clucked to his team, and maneuvered a cautious way ahead through the wild tangle.

Maidie grabbed at his arm. "Hurry, Dad . . . hurry!" she cried. "Everybody will get ahead of us."

Abbott rumbled with laughter. "Easy, lass . . . easy. Gallatin Basin isn't just across that river. It is miles from here, long, weary miles. We got plenty of time. Let the fools fight for a crossing. A lot of them will be finished right here."

Maidie soon saw the truth of this. Wagons were tangled in the river. Some were overturned. Horses were floundering. Men were howling curses at their teams, at each other, at their luck. Gunshots sounded ominously. Women and children were wailing. And no one had a look or a care for the luckless ones. It was strictly a dog-eat-dog proposition, with every man for himself and the devil take the hindmost.

When two wagons tangled wheels short of the river, Jim Abbott saw his chance and swung in ahead of them, into a fording place momentarily open. His team, caught with the virus of excitement, was dancing with eagerness, but Abbott held it down to slow, sure progress, feeling his way across the treacherous boulders under the foaming waters. The wagon lurched from side to side and Maidie clung to the seat with both hands, lips parted, eyes shining. When a deluge of spray, kicked high by the scrambling hoofs of the team, splashed her face and throat, she gasped, then laughed like a delighted child. This was life, raw and savage perhaps, but life and color and action such as she had dreamed about.

Just before they reached the opposite bank, Maidie saw something that struck a cold note into her wildly beating heart. A limp, twisted figure, swirling in the waters, a dark, turgid stain following it. A dead man, followed by the stain of his own blood. Not all of those gunshots had been wild ones.

Then they were across and heading for the rolling hills. Quickly the girl forgot that figure in the water. That, along with the rest of her life, was all behind her now. Ahead lay the promise of a new life in a new land. The tumultuous youth of her reached forward to that future.

Other wagons went rumbling by them, horses on the run. But Jim Abbott did not mind. He kept clear of the reckless ones, held his fretting team to a swinging walk.

Watching the other wagons, Maidie saw one, a little to her left, moving along at the same easy, steady pace as their own. On the box was the roly-poly figure of a Negro, his face all ashine in one huge grin. He caught Maidie's glance and tossed a hand high in greeting. Maidie waved back.

"Dad," she exclaimed. "There goes Mose, Dave Salkeld's cook!"

Jim Abbott nodded. "And using his head, too. Smart rascal. He'll deliver that wagon safe and sound for his boss."

Way out ahead, just speeding dots now against the flanks of the hills, were saddle men. Maidie wondered which of them would be Dave Salkeld and which Lon Estes. For Lon and her father had had a long talk the previous night. It had been agreed that Lon would speed out ahead on horseback, locate the piece of ground he had described, lying along Cache Creek, file on it, then turn his claim over to her father on their arrival.

A strange man, Lon Estes. Maidie thought of how she and her father had come across him, back along the trail into Navajo River Meadows. He had been lying beside that trail, his horse standing over him. At first they had thought him dead, for he carried a wound on his side, a shallow wound, but angry and inflamed from lack of care.

They had gotten him into the wagon and cared for him. Apparently exhaustion and loss of blood had been mainly his trouble. With food and rest and the wounded side properly cared for, his recovery had been amazingly quick. He had offered no explanation for his original condition and neither Maidie nor her father had asked him for one. All he had told them was that he had hunted wild horses in Gallatin Basin and could lead them to some of the best ground in the basin. With this promise in mind they had brought him on to Navajo River Meadows.

Since then he had stayed close to them, rendering them aid in many small ways. Maidie had thought about him a lot, mainly from curiosity. She had never met a man like him before. Even when he was sitting just across the fire from her, he seemed a million miles away, so securely was he locked in his own thoughts.

At times she had caught him watching her intently and she had been a little uneasy. Yet by neither word nor action did he offend in any way. In fact, their first night in the meadows, when a hulking, drunken teamster had grown offensive, Estes had gone at the fellow like an unleashed tiger, knocking him down with a lashing gun barrel and herding him away at the point of that same gun.

Several times Maidie felt as though she would be vastly relieved if Lon Estes would go out of her life as abruptly as he had entered it. But her father seemed to know no worry about the man, so Maidie buried her feelings and was quietly friendly to him. Now it seemed that her father, as usual, had been right. For Lon Estes was speeding far out ahead, to make sure that the Abbotts got possession of some of the best land Gallatin Basin could offer.

There was no uneasiness in Maidie's thoughts when they switched to Dave Salkeld. Instead, there was a quick, glowing warmth. Like Lon Estes, Dave Salkeld was a new type in her life. But there was none of the shadowy, still reticence about him that characterized Estes. Instead, there was an open, stirring virility, a clean, steely, flaming strength and courage that had, for instance, completely crushed a larger, stronger man in Luke Converse and had subdued and routed the Tremper crowd. As she thought of him, all of the glowing color in her cheeks was not that of excitement alone.

The climb up the rolling hills was tedious enough, and Maidie shifted and squirmed on the wagon seat until her father rumbled with laughter. "I know how it is, lass," he said. "You'd like to leap high on swift wings and fly right into Gallatin Basin. So would I. But, being mortal, we have no wings. We just have a sound wagon and a stout, willing team. We'll have to make that combination do."

Maidie felt better when they finally topped the crest of the hills and entered the flat sage country, with out ahead the line of Vermilion Wall beginning to blaze. Here the distance was terrific, but at least one could mark some progress.

All that long day the sage rolled by on either side of the slowly wheeling wagon. Heat came down and rolls of sweat foam gathered about the harness on the team. Maidie donned a sunbonnet and set out to prove to her father that she had in her the stuff of which the true pioneer was made.

At midday they stopped for a time. Maidie helped her father unhitch the team, which was then rubbed down vigorously with pieces of burlap sacking. After which each horse was given one bucket full of precious water from the water keg and a little later a nosebag full of equally precious grain, which Jim Abbott had hoarded jealously from the very beginning of the long trip from the old home.

Had this stop been made earlier in the day, Maidie would have been wild with impatience. But by this time she had begun to see plenty of evidence of her father's good judgment. Wagons that had sped recklessly out ahead of them were now dropping back, teams exhausted from overdriving. She saw several outfits where at least one and sometimes both horses were down, to the despair of the owners.

Jim Abbott caught the thoughtful look in her eye and shrugged. "I feel sorry for them, too, lass," he rumbled. "But there is nothing we can do for them. They are victims of their own folly."

They drove the scorching afternoon out and, with ponderous, mocking slowness, the great flaming wall ahead of them drew closer, towering ever higher. Straining her eyes, Maidie could see tiny dots that were horsemen riding straight into that great wall, seemingly to be swallowed up by the sheer bulwark of blazing sandstone.

"We'll never get by there today, Dad," she said.

"Never expected to," said her father comfortably. "Lon Estes told me all about that Vermilion Wall. It is cut through by what is known as Antelope Pass, and Lon said, come nightfall, there is a queer wind blows through that pass, a regular cyclone, full of sand and hell. It would be suicide trying to go through against that wind, Lon said. So I figured all along to camp just this side the wall and go through first thing in the morning."

In a savagely beautiful twilight, the Abbott wagon reached the wall, at the northern entrance of Antelope Pass. Already that wind was blowing. It came whistling through the pass, freighted with fine, cutting particles of sand. Jim Abbott pulled away to a spot right under the Vermilion Wall, but a good 200 yards from the mouth of the pass. Here they were within sound of that wind, but away from any touch of it, and here they made camp.

Another wagon that had been following closely behind them pulled over and stopped nearby. A big, hearty voice hailed them. It was Mose.

"You folks are right smart people!" he called. "And this darky ain't wantin' any of that debbil wind."

Other wagons gathered, some which had tried the pass and had to turn back before the rising fury of the wind. Soon there were scores of camps, the crimson eyes of campfires winking, pungent sage smoke swirling and rising.

After supper, Mose came over to the Abbott fire with his banjo, to strum and sing a while. Maidie was amazed how comforting it was to have this cheerful old fellow so close at hand.

Mose did not linger overly long. Weariness lay heavily on these wagon people. It had been a hard day. Fires burned low, became little heaps of dusty jewels, then only cold ashes. As usual, Jim Abbott spread his sougan under the wagon, which left the wagon to Maidie.

At first Maidie was unable to sleep and she lay wide-eyed, listening to the distant roar and wail of the wind through Antelope Pass, thrilled to the pulse of this wild and savagely beautiful land—this new frontier that held the secret of her future. It was the never-ending drone of the wind that finally lulled her to sleep.

Hours later, in the black heart of the night, she awakened

with a start. Under the wagon there was a struggle going on. She heard the bewildered roar of her father, then a thin voice cursing, the sound of a sodden blow, and a groan. Then the sand-muffled sound of running footsteps. Then silence. Another groan and the voice of her father, calling weakly: "Maidie . . . Maidie, lass! They've knifed me!"

Heart in her mouth, Maidie scrambled from the wagon. In the whitely brilliant star shine, she saw her father beside a wagon wheel, trying to drag himself erect. He got to his feet finally, stood there swaying. Maidie caught him in her arms, sobbing: "Dad! Oh, Dad . . . what is it?"

"Some creeping devil with a knife," said Jim Abbott thickly. "He caught me in my blankets. He was feeling for my throat when I woke up. I grabbed at him and we had a tussle. Then he drove a knife into me. He was trying for my heart, but I was rolling at the time and he got me in the shoulder. I'm bleeding . . . bad."

Maidie felt the weakness of him and forced him to lie down. Then she sped to that closest wagon. "Mose!" she cried. "Mose . . . come quick! My father . . . he's been hurt!"

There was a sleepy mumbling, then Mose popped his kinky head out of the wagon. "That yo', li'l missy? You say yo' pappy is hurt? Mose be right there."

Maidie sped back to her father, dragged his blankets from under the wagon, and got him on top of them. Then Mose was beside her, a candle lantern in his hand.

In jerky sentences, Maidie told Mose what had happened, and the kindly old fellow got to work immediately. He bared the wound, looked it over, and drew a big sigh of relief. "Yo' pap's gwine be all right, honey chile," he said gently. "Yo' get Mose some water and clean cloth and we soon stop that bleedin'."

Maidie brought Mose what he asked for, and her father was soon as comfortable as could be expected. "Take holt of me, boss," said Mose. " 'Spect from here on in to Gallatin Basin yo'll rest easy in the wagon, while li'l missy does the drivin'. And Mose will stay right with yo', to make sho' yo' git there safe and sound."

With Jim Abbott resting on Maidie's sougan, Mose climbed out of the wagon and took a squint at the stars. "Night 'most gone," he announced. "Ole Mose jest got time to git his old shotgun an' take a li'l prowl. An' should he see any no-account trash sneakin' around, he pepper 'em good, sho' nuff. I be back soon, missy."

They heard the honest old fellow move away. Maidie found her father's hand and clung to it. "Oh, Dad," she gulped. "After . . . after this . . . I'm going to hate this new country."

"No, you're not," said Jim Abbott. "Anything worthwhile having is worth fighting for. But can you handle the team from here on in?"

Maidie tossed her head. "Of course I can. Don't worry about that. But, Dad . . . who could have done this to you . . . and why?"

Jim Abbott was silent for a moment. "In the dark, I couldn't tell a thing," he said slowly. "Yet there was something about the fellow, a thin, stringy, wildcat something . . . that made me think of the Trempers. And I can't think of anyone else who would have a grudge against me."

"Those filthy Trempers!" exploded Maidie. "Why are there such people in the world? All they do is cause trouble."

"Aye, they cause trouble. But in the end they write their own finish. They always do. And you'll find that the Trempers will do the same, one of these days. Now you better get some more rest, lass."

"No," said Maidie determinedly. "I couldn't. Anyway, Mose said it was nearly morning. We'll soon be rolling again, Dad."

"That fellow," said Jim Abbott. "He's pure gold."

A half hour later, Mose came back. "That coyote done holed up, I 'spect," he reported. "Good thing for him, he did. Well, east is turnin' gray, missy. You eat yo' breakfast with Mose, and then we get all ready to roll. Better times ahead."

Maidie found one of Mose's fists and pressed it. "You're awful sweet, Mose."

"Ho, ho!" chortled Mose. "I'se jest a harum-scarum black fellow who likes to see people happy. Breakfast be ready in a jiffy."

He hurried away. Maidie stared thoughtfully through the slow-stealing dawn. "Harum-scarum black fellow," she said to herself, "but with the biggest and whitest heart in the world."

CHAPTER SEVEN

Through a pearl gray, dew-wet morning, Dave Salkeld and his men drove out into Gallatin Basin. Just at sunup they cleared the timberland in which they had camped and ahead of them lay vast miles of open, rolling grassland, which finally flowed into the flanks of a distant, lonely range of black, timber-clad mountains. South and west the basin ran away into distance, still shrouded with morning mists. In back of them, rearing above the timber and the strip of sage beyond, was the rampart of Vermilion Wall, beginning to burn in the first light of the sun. This end of Antelope Pass was a blot of shadow, and now, moving out of that shadow into the sunlight, crept a tiny dot.

Dirk Bender whooped. "There's the first wagon! You got to hand it to them wagon folks. I've cussed 'em plenty in the past when I've seen 'em clutter up and spoil good cattle range, but danged if they ain't a stout lot. When they set their minds to a thing, they shore got what it takes. Makes a feller swell up sort of proud of his country and the people in it."

Dave Salkeld set his course due east, with a sugar-loaf peak of the distant mountains directly over his bronco's ears. Then it was just ride and ride. Lon Estes rode with them, still keeping his silence, face stoic and unchanging.

Hidden here and there in the rolling grasslands they crossed little creeks, lined with the crisp green of willow and alder. Along these watercourses would the wagon folks settle. Here rude cabins would be built, acres fenced, and the steel nose of the plow bite into virgin soil. This whole great basin would have made a cattle empire such as men might dream of, but Dave Salkeld knew that such a dream could never be realized now.

Long ago he had learned that it brought no profit to a man to try and fight the inevitable. The wagon man, the hoe man, the squatter would come. To try and fight him forever was a losing battle. The wise cattleman would no longer waste his strength and substance trying to stem the ever-rising tide. Instead, he sought out range above the limits of that tide. Such was Dave's aim now.

In time, off to their right, they glimpsed a few threads of pale blue smoke. "Boardman's Flat," explained Dave to his riders. "Buck Custer and I stopped there for a while when we were in this basin a month ago, lining up our range. It used to be a wilderness trading post, kept alive by trappers, wild horse hunters, and some Indian trade. Now it will be a town. The Land Office has been set up there."

In time the slope of the basin was up, reaching closer and closer to the range of timbered mountains. Here they came upon the rushing waters of the largest creek they had yet crossed.

"Cache Creek," said Dave. "We go on up it."

Lon Estes spoke for the first time. "I'm leaving you here, Salkeld. I'll see that you get your bronc' back."

"Any time," said Dave. "Good luck."

Estes turned downcreek, Dave and his men up. Tonto Rice moved in by Dave. "Who is that *hombre*, Dave?"

"Name is Lon Estes. A friend, it seems, of Jim Abbott."

"I've seen my share of tough ones," said Tonto. "I never saw one any harder than that gent."

Cache Creek climbed the slope of country rapidly. In time it forked and Dave took the right-hand branch, which foamed through a short, abrupt cañon; above the cañon the range widened out into a great benchland, roughly diamond-shaped, with timbered hills walling it in. The creek split the center of the diamond, flowing out of a gorge in the mountains that was guarded by a single spire of maroon and yellow sandstone.

Dave pointed. "All right, Jumbo and Dirk. That's Painted Rock. Go ride your sections out, one on each side of the creek. Make 'em long and narrow, so you take in plenty of creekbank. Pudge, you and Wampus cut up east of that rock. You'll find a big open basin up there with a timber island right in the middle of it. In that timber is a big spring. We want control of that spring. Ride your claims and set your monuments. We'll wait down here for you. Tonto, we'll throw our claims adjoining Jumbo and Dirk on this lower end."

Crude calculations were made, stakes cut and driven, notices written and set up. While they waited for the return of Pudge and Wampus, Dave pointed out the advantages of their new range.

"We got summer and winter range. We got year-around water. There's no end of logs in the timber for building. Buck Custer and me rode this basin for three long weeks, prying into every corner of it, and this is the place we picked. Converse can have whatever else he can find, but this stretch is ours, and we hold it, come hell or high water."

Pudge and Wampus reported back from the upper range, wildly enthused. "Sweetest piece of summer range up there I ever saw," said Pudge. "You and Buck got something here, boss."

"We all got something," corrected Dave quietly. "Buck and me, we've decided to cut you boys in on a percentage of the profits. You're all joint owners of the Flying Diamond brand from here on out."

The riders were stunned. Here was something revolutionary in the cattle game. No longer just $40 and found. They were part owners in a real brand now. They sputtered and stuttered and marveled.

Dave smiled grimly. "We've got a fight ahead of us. It won't take Converse long to realize he's played his cards wrong. The majority of the settlers will beat that herd of his into the basin. They'll have all of the main basin gobbled up. Being Converse, he'll try and run 'em out. He won't have a mite of luck, for he can't whip 'em. Then he'll come at us. You'll find that owning an interest in a brand is different than just drawing wages. You'll have to work harder and fight harder than ever before. You can't quit and go drifting when your feet get itchy. You've got real responsibilities now, you worthless saddle pounders."

"Responsibilities!" bawled Jumbo. "We'll eat 'em up. Come on . . . let's get to the Land Office and file these claims. I feel as important as hell. By gollies, I do, for a fact."

They spurred off, whooping. Dave took a more leisurely pace. Tonto rode with him. "You and Buck have made a mighty generous move, Dave," said Tonto.

Dave shrugged. "Why not? We've got a good, faithful crew. The boys deserve a break. Buck and me started playing with the idea a full year ago. We started watching the boys, figuring which of them was worth it. We weeded out a couple, Río Hocken and Buzz Winter, if you remember."

"I remember." Tonto nodded. "And they went right over and hired out with Converse. So that was why you let 'em go. I often wondered."

"That was why," said Dave.

Boardman's Flat had originally been made up of a couple of log buildings and some straggling corrals. It had been lonely, sleepy, little frequented. Old Bill Boardman had eked out a meager living, trading with trappers, wild horse hunters, and a few wandering bands of Indians. Now the pulse-quickening throb of new blood, new life had taken hold. The two buildings had increased to twelve, the newly peeled logs of which glinted in the sunlight. Two of those buildings were saloons, open for business, stocked with liquor brought in by pack train across the Windy Mountains to the east. A newly arrived pack train stood in front of one of the places and men were unloading the animals.

The Land Office had been set up in one corner of Boardman's original trading post, and there Dave and his men filed their claims. The land agent, a thin, tall, sharp-faced man with shrewd blue eyes, spoke crisply.

"You fellows are the first. How'd you make such good time?"

"By saddle," drawled Dave. "And each man with a relay of spare bronc's."

"Not for speculation, I hope," warned the agent. "We won't stand for that sort of thing."

"Mister," bawled Jumbo, "we'll be right here in Gallatin Basin, earning an honest living on that land when you're a grandfather."

The agent laughed. "That's the spirit, cowboy."

As they went out the door, Jumbo gave Dirk Bender a mighty slap on the back. "Well, Mister Bender, what do you think of yourself about now? You got a toehold on a real piece of earth. For the first time in your life you own something more than the clothes on your back and your saddle. How does it feel to be a bloated landowner?"

Dirk coughed until he got his breath back. "I feel like I'm going to take another bloated landowner plumb apart if you don't keep those big mitts to yourself. Hell's heat! You just about put a crook in my back bone, you damned big ape."

"Lookit!" yelped Wampus. "Here comes the first of the wagon men. And still crazy as bedbugs."

Two riders swung into the clear, coming down the rude street at a wild, clumsy gallop. The horses they bestrode were gaunt and ready to drop, heavy, slow animals fashioned more for pulling a plow than carrying men in a race. Both animals were heavy with flapping, jangling harness.

Side-by-side they came tearing on, each determined to beat the other to the Land Office. They were cursing one another and shaking fists as they rode. When the horses came to a heavy, exhausted stop, the men piled off and sped for the Land Office door. They struck it together, wedged there, and began to fight.

They went down, rolling over and over in a wild tangle, grunting and cursing and swinging heavy, clumsy fists.

"*Whoopee!*" howled Wampus. "Claw him, brother . . . claw him! You ain't got much time. Only a hundred years or so."

One of the fighters managed to land a lucky blow that partially stunned the other. The victor scrambled to his feet and lunged for the door, only to have the victim make a blind grab, catch a booted ankle, and spill the owner of the ankle with a crash. Then the partially stunned one went through the door, crawling on hands and knees.

The Flying Diamond boys went into hysterics. Wampus rolled on the earth, kicking his feet in the air in a frenzy of delight. Jumbo clung to the side of the trading post, in a bellow of mirth that could be heard a mile away.

"Haw, haw, haw! He made it. He had to finish crawlin' on his belly, but he got there first. He made it. Haw, haw, haw."

The tripped one got slowly up, stared at the cowboys like a dazed owl, then stumbled into the Land Office. Dirk and Pudge wrapped arms about each other and wept with glee. Even old Tonto Rice cackled thinly.

Dave laughed with the rest. It had been funny enough, but it was merely another proof of the hysteria of the land rush.

Another rider showed up, coming at a leisurely jog. It was Lon Estes. He nodded curtly as he dismounted and began stripping his saddle from the bronco Dave had loaned him.

"No rush about returning the horse, Estes," said Dave.

ning and crowding about. To the volley of questions, the man with the shotgun stated his case in flat, cold, emotionless words.

"He killed one of my broncos," he rasped. "What was I to do, tell him to go ahead and kill the rest?"

The crowd was callous, quickly deciding that the killing was justified. The dead man was dragged from the center of the street, to await burial when someone found time to get around to the chore. And the raw, brutal rush of life went on.

"There's the start of a boothill for you, Dave," said Tonto. "And there'll be more, a lot more, before things quiet down. I knew it."

"Let's get back to the corrals," suggested Dave. "Temperatures are running a little too high around here to suit me. No telling when some wild *hombre* will decide he don't like the way we wear our hats and set out to do something about it. And we came into the basin to raise cattle, not to act as targets for some whiskey-muddled wagon man."

Steadily the stream of wagons rolling in thickened. Horses, wagons, people—all showed the effects of the wild race in from the Navajo River Meadows. Men were gaunt and sunken of eye, but still burning with the fever of the rush. Deathly weary women hunched on the hard wagon seats beside their men, some holding children in their arms.

"What was the shooting about?" asked Jumbo, when Dave and Tonto got back to the corral. "Last shot sounded like a powder keg had blowed up."

"That last shot was two of them," answered Dave grimly. "Both barrels of a shotgun at close range. Boardman's Flat has got a start for its boothill." He went on to detail the shooting scrape.

Jumbo shook a ponderous head. "This civilization thing don't reach very deep," he philosophized. "No sense to a killing like that. But you get a man all excited, pour some liquor into him,

and then scratch him, and you find the savage mighty close under the surface."

They lounged at ease about the corral, while the afternoon hours slipped away and the unbroken stream of wagons still came flowing in. Wampus stirred restlessly. "I hope Mose don't travel too darned leisurely. Me, I'm anxious to get out to my new range and start setting my roots."

"Listen to him," snorted Jumbo. "*His* range. My, oh, my . . . how important some young squirts can get."

"Well, some of it is mine," defended Wampus. "Ain't that right, Dave? Ain't it?"

"Sure it is, kid." Dave grinned. "From now on and forever more. Don't you let 'em bluff you out."

"I ain't going to," said Wampus stoutly. "Not even a big, slab-sided ape like Mister Jumbo Curtis can run a shindy on me. I'm a landowner and I'll stick to it, sink, swim, or suck eggs."

"Hey!" exclaimed Pudge. "There's the Abbott wagon . . . and the girl is driving."

Dave jumped to his feet. The wagon was rolling in slowly. At the reins was a slim figure in overalls and hickory shirt, still subtly graceful despite the evident weariness in the sagging shoulders and the formlessness of rude clothes. Looking at her, Dave sensed something far more wrong than just that cloak of weariness.

"Something has happened to Jim Abbott!" he exclaimed. "Else he'd be at those reins." Dave vaulted the fence and hurried over to the wagon. "Maidie!" he called. "Maidie Abbott, where's your father?"

She pulled the wagon out of line and set the brakes. The smile she gave him was wan and tired. "He's in the wagon, hurt. Last night we camped the other side of that terrible Vermilion Wall. There were a lot of others camped there, too. During the night someone tried to . . . to knife Dad. He woke

up and fought them off, but they left him with a badly cut shoulder."

Dave's face went taut. "The Tremper outfit?" he asked.

Her shrug was eloquent. "We can't be sure, of course. But the Tremper wagon was camped there. And I don't know of anyone else who would have anything against Dad. Your man, Mose . . . has been very good to us. He helped doctor Dad and he's kept behind me all the way in, to make sure I got here. He'll be close behind right now. Have you seen Lon Estes?"

"He's around town here somewhere. I'll hunt him up for you, if you wish."

She nodded, incredibly tired. "If you would. I'd . . . we'd appreciate it a lot, Dad and I."

"You bet!" Dave exclaimed. "You might as well wait right here. You couldn't drive that wagon down the street now without an army corps to help you."

Dave fought his way through the human maëlstrom that had engulfed Boardman's Flat, looking for the lithe, thin-faced figure of the gunman. He still could not understand the tie between this obviously desperate character and the Abbotts, father and daughter. But he did not bother now to try and figure it out. He'd promised to locate Estes and he meant to do it.

His search was finally successful in the new tent eating house. Estes had evidently just finished his meal, for he was pushing his way out of the narrow, confined space, building a thin cigarette.

"The Abbotts have arrived," Dave told him bluntly. "Jim Abbott's been hurt. Somebody tried to knife him last night in the camp beyond Vermilion Wall. Miss Abbott sent me after you."

Pinpoints of crimson flickered in the gunman's hard eyes. He spoke one word, thin and cold: "Trempers?"

"Miss Abbott said she wasn't shore. But it was likely them. Come on."

When they got back to the wagon, they found Tonto inside, looking at Jim Abbott's wounds. Tonto had just called to Wampus: "Get along and ask Bill Boardman if he's got some balsam oil around the place! Likely he's traded to the Indians for some at one time or another. There ain't nothin' can touch balsam oil when it comes to healing."

Wampus hurried off. Lon Estes crawled into the wagon. "Who did it, Jim?" he asked.

Abbott lifted a feverish face. "That part don't matter now, Lon. Did you take care of that other business?"

Estes nodded. "Posted and filed. The chunk of land I told you about. We're all set there." Then, going back to his first query: "Was it that Tremper crowd?"

"Don't know for shore," answered Abbott. "It was black dark. I was too busy fighting the whelp off to get a chance to recognize him. It wasn't that I was worrying about. It was the land. Now we got that safe, I feel better."

Jim Abbott's wounds were both on his left shoulder, long, angry knife cuts that had been aimed at his heart but had been deflected by bone and heavy muscle. He had lost enough blood to leave him weak and pallid-looking.

"I'm wondering if there's some kind of a doctor to be located in this damn' town," said Lon Estes tensely.

"We can look," said Dave Salkeld. "But I doubt it. Anyway, Tonto is just about as good at this sort of thing as anybody I know. He'll do a job."

Jumbo Curtis stuck his head over the tailgate, lifting in a dripping canteen. "How'd a drink of fresh cold water go?" he boomed, trying fruitlessly to keep his big voice down to ordinary conversation level.

"Swell," said Abbott thickly.

He nearly drained the canteen, then sank back with a sigh. "That was good," he murmured. "Good."

Wampus came rushing back, carrying a quart whiskey bottle full of a dark, amber fluid, oily and pungent. "Here's the very thing you asked for, Tonto," he panted.

"Keno!" exclaimed Tonto. "We'll fix you up now, Abbott. This stuff will heal anything."

Tonto smeared the angry wounds liberally with the cooling, aromatic oil, then bound them securely with strips of clean, white cloth that the girl supplied. He left the bottle with Maidie. "Tomorrow about this time you put on another smear of that oil, miss. Do that once a day for the next week and there won't be a thing left but the scars."

Maidie looked at Dave and Tonto and the other Flying Diamond boys with moist eyes. "Thank you," she said, her voice low. "Thank you all . . . so much. You've been . . . very kind."

"Glad to have been of help," said Dave. "You say Mose isn't far behind?"

"He can't be very far. Lon, do you think we ought to go on to our land tonight?"

The gunman shook his head. "No need. It'll be there in the morning. And the team looks pretty much played out. We'll leave first thing in the morning."

"But suppose somebody else has settled there?"

Estes shrugged. "They'll leave again. Don't worry."

Dave and his riders returned to their perches on the corral fence. Estes unhitched the weary Abbott team and tied them to the wagon wheels, then began rustling wood for a fire. Other wagons pulling up, finding it little use to try and get any closer to the center of town, began pitching camp.

Blue twilight settled over Gallatin Basin. The air was cool and pleasant. Wampus stirred again. "Where the deuce is Mose?" he stewed. "Wonder if anything could have happened to him on the homestretch?"

"Naw," grunted Jumbo. "That happy-go-lucky cuss has got

just one speed and you couldn't jar him out of it with a hunk of dynamite. He'll be along."

"Listen!" exclaimed Dirk.

Cutting through the clamor of the flat came the sound of a cheerful, mellow voice raised in song:

> Come along, yo' hungry cowboys, an' git yo'
> victuals hot,
> You'll find fat meat in the fryin' pan an' taters in
> the pot.

"That's him!" yelped Wampus. "Come on."

They found Mose pulling in just at the outskirts of the wagon crush. Through a mask of dust, Mose looked all rolling eyes and flashing white teeth.

"Here I is, Marse Dave." He grinned. "You boys take care of them broncos and Mose'll have yo' supper ready in two jiffs."

"No you don't, you good old chunk of midnight!" bawled Jumbo. "You just stretch out and rest yourself. I'll do the cookin' tonight. Dirk, go rustle a couple of buckets of fresh water. Wampus, you and Pudge scare up some firewood."

Dave and Tonto began unhitching the team.

"Ain't only cookin' that Mose is wise at," observed Tonto. "Look at these bronc's, Dave. They're in better shape than any team I've seen roll in from that drive."

"Mose rates up," said Dave. "He gets his share in the outfit, too."

When water and firewood showed up, Mose asserted his authority. "Yo' shoo 'way," he told Jumbo. "Ain't nobody in this outfit can cook real victuals but Mose. I don't need no rest. I'se jest bustin' to go. Shoo 'way and give me room."

Mose won his argument and soon had a hot meal ready. "Marse Dave . . . did that li'l missy Abbott and her pappy git here all safe?" he asked.

Dave nodded. "She told me how you'd helped them out. Do you think it was one of that Tremper crowd who tried to knife Jim Abbott?"

Mose shrugged. "I 'spect, Marse Dave. Can't say for sho', though. When that li'l missy came runnin' to Mose like a li'l scared pickaninny, I helped her first git her pappy bandaged. Then I took my ol' shotgun and made me a prowl all 'round that camp. The Tremper wagon was there, but I couldn't find nobody sneakin' around."

"Suppose you had, Mose," wondered Wampus. "What would you have done?"

"Huh!" sniffed Mose. "Yo' ask what I'd've done, curly haid? I'd jest spread me a flock of buckshot all over a square mile of ground, that's what I'd've done. You got no idea what a woolly wolf ol' Mose can be when he git stirred up an' shootin' mad."

"So Miss Abbott had to drive their wagon all the way from beyond Vermilion Wall, eh?" said Dave.

Mose beamed. "She had to and she did, Marse Dave. Mose, he trailed along behind and kept an eye on her, case she got into trouble. But she didn't. No, sir! She came right on through, jest like she been drivin' wagons all her life. She sho' is one stout li'l muggins."

The meal over, Dave sent Wampus and Dirk and Pudge to the corrals to get their saddle mounts and tether them to the wagon for the night. "Too late to go out to the range now," he said. "And we want to be sure we got our bronc's in the morning."

After which, Dave and Tonto headed up to town again. On their way they passed the Abbott wagon, which was dark and silent. Evidently Maidie and her father were already asleep. There was no sign of Lon Estes.

Night had not changed or lessened the confusion in Boardman's Flat. With every passing hour the jam grew thicker and noisier. Tents had sprung up everywhere. Many of them housed some kind of a beginning business. The crowd that jostled up and down the street was almost wholly made up of men now. They were noisy, unruly, simmering with excitement. Liquor flowed freely, too freely. The air was explosive, ripe for any kind of violence.

A haggard, disheveled man pushed his way out of the Land Office door, slamming and locking the door behind him. He waved his arms to quiet the howl of protest that went up. It was Castner, the land agent.

"That's positively all for tonight!" he yelled hoarsely. "I'm all in. I ain't had a bite to eat since morning. I got to get some rest. I'll be back on the job tomorrow."

Despite the pleas, curses, and even threats, he pushed through the crowd and disappeared. The disappointed ones turned to the saloons for consolation.

In the trading post Dave and Tonto found Bill Boardman staring dazedly at his barren shelves. "Just like a plague of katydids," mumbled the trader. "Just like a prairie fire. I ain't got a thing left to sell. And it'll be worse tomorrow. If I only had an idea it would be like this. Well, there ain't a thing I can do but wait until that pack train gets in from Aspen City."

The two main saloons were crowded to suffocation. Men lined the bars eight and ten deep. A fat, red-faced, sweating man grabbed Dave by the arm. "Listen, cowboy," he panted. "I own this place. I'll pay you twenty dollars a day if you'll head for Aspen City, get together a pack train, and bring me in all the liquor you can round up. This is the thirstiest gang I ever met up with. My bartenders are just about to the bottom of the kegs. I'll have to close my doors if I don't get a fresh supply of liquor somewhere."

"Sorry," said Dave. "I got business of my own to attend to."

The fat man cursed his disappointment and scurried off, trying to line up help somewhere else.

Poker games were going full blast and at several of the tables the inevitable professional gamblers were in evidence, somber in garb, with cold, white, predatory faces.

"Those tinhorns," murmured Tonto. "They always manage to show up in a town like this. They always make me think of a flock of buzzards coming in to a feast. One minute there ain't a sign of one. And then, all of a sudden out of nowhere, the sky is full of 'em. Look, Dave . . . there's Lon Estes."

The gunman was standing beside one of the poker tables, watching the turn of the cards. From time to time his hard eyes would lift and flicker toward the door of the place. It was as though he was waiting and watching for the arrival of someone.

Even as Dave looked at the gunman, he saw Estes's flickering glance go to the doorway once again. Dave saw that glance settle into a crimson gleam while a queer tautness struck all through the gunman's lithe body. Then Estes, swiftly prowling, was headed for the door.

Just forcing a way through the crowd about the doorway was a lank, hatchet-faced figure, lips sagging in eagerness to get to the bar and the whiskey being sold over it. It was one of the Trempers. Lon Estes was descending on the man like a darting hawk.

"Get out of line, Tonto," hissed Dave. "Hell's going to pop."

CHAPTER EIGHT

The thirsty member of the Tremper family did not see Lon Estes until the gunman caught him by the arm and swung him around. Neither Dave nor Tonto could hear what it was that Estes said to the hatchet-faced renegade, but, whatever it was, it made Tremper jerk back, cursing, while his darting hand flicked a knife from inside the front of his greasy shirt. He made one lightning pass at Estes, ripping a crimson furrow across the back of the hand Estes threw up in defense. Then Estes flashed a gun and shot his man through the heart. Tremper gasped and collapsed.

The report of the gun rumbled through the saloon, bringing a moment of wild confusion as men surged about, trying to get out of line. But as no second shot followed, a strained silence fell over the place, a silence broken only by the hard, gusty breathing of startled men.

A cleared space had appeared magically, leaving Lon Estes in the open, standing over the body of his victim. Estes swung slowly around, naked gun and narrowed glittering eyes stabbing and measuring all the rest of the room and crowd. His voice ran over the room with a thin, hissing note: "He was one of a litter of skunks who tried to knife a good man in his blankets. Anybody got any objections they want to follow up?"

A member of the crowd spoke explosively. "Hell, no! A knife man is one of the devil's own. Let the devil take him!"

Estes nodded, prowled to the door, and was gone. The room

took on a rising clamor as men crowded to look at the twisted ugliness of violent death. Dave and Tonto followed Estes into the night.

"Number two," said Tonto cynically. "And the night is still a pup. No boom town boothill ever got a better start than Boardman's Flat, Dave."

Dave nodded soberly. "That Lon Estes is a wolf, for a fact. But I doubt the wisdom of that play, unless he figures to follow it up until he's wiped out the whole Tremper gang. Because the rest of the Trempers will connect him with Jim and Maidie Abbott, and, as long as a Tremper is left alive, there'll be a dirty threat hanging over the Abbotts."

"When a gunfighter goes on the peck," said Tonto sagely, "he don't stop to do much thinking. Yet Estes ain't the only man who is going to throw lead before Gallatin Basin turns law-minded. We're liable to have to do our share of the same."

"Maybe," said Dave thinly. "Look yonder. There is Converse and some of his men."

In the flare of light coming from the open door of Bill Boardman's trading post, the shadowy figures of four riders were dismounting. "Converse, Slim Jepson, Bob Chehallis, and Saugus Lee," said Tonto. "Wonder what brings them to town? And where their herd is?"

"Maybe we can find out," said Dave grimly. "Come on."

They sauntered into the trading post. Converse was arguing with Bill Boardman, who had spread his hands helplessly.

"Not my fault, mister," Boardman was saying. "I'm waiting for more supplies. Right now I ain't got a quart of flour, let alone half a dozen sacks. This crazy gang of boomers has cleaned my shelves right down to the bare boards. Sorry."

Converse, cursing bitterly, turned away and his black, sullen eyes fell on Dave and Tonto. Converse's face still showed some of the effects of his fight with Dave, back at Navajo River

Meadows. His lips curled.

"Well, look who's here. Mister Salkeld and Mister Rice, looking smug as you please. I thought you and Custer were bringing a herd into Gallatin, Salkeld."

"You know damn' well we are," Dave shot back. "You tried your damnedest to have it stampeded at Tunison Wells, if you remember. And we'll bring it in, in our own good time."

Converse's laugh was short and ugly. "Then you better hurry. Else there'll be no range left. The boomers have shore hit this basin like a swarm of ants. Every creek in the basin is lined with wagons."

Dave shrugged. "Buck and me ain't worrying. We've got our range."

Converse's black eyes flickered. "Where?" he snapped.

Dave shrugged again. "Right now you'll have to guess. We played our cards smarter than you, Converse. We got our range first. Now, when we bring in our herd, we'll have a place to put it. And we aim to hold that range, come hell or high water. Don't you ever forget that, Converse . . . in case you get ideas."

Converse hunched his heavy shoulders forward. "You making war talk, Salkeld?"

"Take it that way if you want. After that dirty trick you tried to pull at Tunison Wells, Buck and me are ready for anything. Anything you send our way will be met right on the nose."

"Keno," snarled Converse. "I reckon we understand each other. Now I'll tell you something. Any range in this basin that the Cross C happens to like is the range we take. Now you know. All right, boys . . . let's drift. We had our ride for nothing. Looks like we eat straight meat until this fool trader gets some more supplies in."

Converse went out with his old, arrogant swagger, his scowling riders crowding after him. Dave and Tonto watched the door alertly until hoofs *clattered* away in the night. Bill Boardman spoke, growling: "Pretty heavy-mouthed, that *hombre*. Who does he think he is, God Almighty?"

The Flying Diamond outfit pulled out of Boardman's Flat in the cool grayness of early dawn. Dave Salkeld had a little argument with himself, then sent Tonto Rice over to the Abbott wagon.

"See if you can find out how Jim Abbott is making it," he said.

Tonto looked at him a little shrewdly, then *clanked* away. Dave felt a little foolish about it, but he could not put aside a certain pique that had gripped him. It rose from the fact that Maidie Abbott seemed to place so much reliance on the gunman, Lon Estes. That, of course, was her own business. Yet for the life of him, Dave could not reconcile any connection between a spirited, wholesome girl like Maidie Abbott and this sultry, venomous gunfighter.

Dave knew his West as well as any man, for he had spent his whole life along the wild frontier. It was an elemental, fierce land and it fashioned men to its own ends. Many times force was the only solution to a problem. Men fought each other and, at times, killed each other. Sometimes they had to kill to survive, or to protect their honest interests. Dave himself had known a couple of those tense, furious moments when he had had to rely on his speed of hand and eye, to go on living. He had seen men go down before his guns, never to rise again. Such things were a phase of the country and life, regrettable but insistent.

Yet there was a difference between a man who fought only to protect himself or honest interests and one who prowled along the edges of honest achievement, his only trade that of killing. Such men were accorded a certain respect, the respect of fear. They were human wolves, fattening only on their reputations for deadliness. In them, at all times, burned the feral spark that only the blood of another victim could momentarily quench. Dave could not understand such a perversion, but he knew the victim of the fever when he saw one. Such was this Lon Estes, with his thin, hard face, his peculiar eyes in which the crimson burned when the killing urge was on him. What justifiable connection could there be between a girl like Maidie Abbott and a man like Lon Estes.

It wasn't just the killing of one of the Tremper crowd. It was all the marks of his deadly trade that had shown in Estes as he went about the fateful job. Perhaps Tremper deserved killing. He was one of a worthless, venomous family. Yet a sound thrashing might have served the purpose just as well. It would not have centered the hatred of the rest of the Tremper family on Jim and Maidie Abbott, as the killing was sure to do. But Lon Estes had waited for his man, knowing what he intended to do, and then going ruthlessly through with it. The unmistakable mark of the killer.

Tonto Rice came back. "Abbott is a lot better," he reported. "His fever is gone. He'll be as good as new shortly. The girl was up, getting the wagon ready to roll. Estes was there, helping her."

"Fair enough," said Dave brusquely. "Let's ride."

They set their pace to that of Mose and the wagon, moving out across the rolling grass country directly for their chosen range on Cache Creek.

All along the route they saw wagons, pulled up in camp. Most were along the several watercourses, while others, unable to find a piece of unoccupied land along the water, had staked their claims farther back. And still the tide came pouring in. In every direction were wagons creeping along, drivers surveying the range hungrily, torn with indecision as to whether to stop and settle where they were, or to go on in further search of acres more closely allied to their dreams.

Right now, greed and suspicion were still rampant forces. It would not be until later, when all the basin was settled and men began to feel secure in their holdings, that the better traits of human nature would begin to show, when neighborliness and friendly communion with their fellows would become dominant forces among them.

Those who had already made their selection of land watched the passing of other wagons in cold suspicion, a weapon of some kind always within reach. Particularly toward Dave and his men did this suspicion and dislike show. For they were patently cowmen, and from the beginning of the West, the hoe man, the squatter, the sodbuster had been at sword's point with the cattlemen.

"Pretty soon," said Wampus, "I'm going to get the idea that these land-hungry johnnies got no more use for us than they would a stripy skunk. Did you see that last jasper? He had one hand on a whiffletree and the other on a big Sharps buff' gun."

"Didn't I always say you had the look of a boogie man?" joked Jumbo. "Now, didn't I?"

Wampus was the youngest of the outfit, hardly past his majority, with a chubby, boyish, freckled face, his outstanding appearance being that of an overgrown, bashful kid. He looked at Jumbo uncertainly. "I think you're funnin' me," he said, getting red in the face.

"Me!" exclaimed Jumbo virtuously. "Why, I wouldn't do that to you, Wampus."

The rest of the outfit chuckled.

"*Aw!*" blurted Wampus. "*Aw-w!*"

They passed one group of three wagons, obviously all of one party. Big wagons, loaded to a heavy, creaking ponderousness, each drawn by a six-horse team, and loaded with a miscellany of machinery. The outfit was headed for the nearest of the timber slopes of the Windy Mountains.

"Whoever owns that rig is a smart man," said Dave. "He's not worrying about grabbing off a chunk of farming land. And he'll make more money than all the rest combined. That's sawmill machinery and yonder in the mountains is all the timber he wants for the taking. And folks will pay high for sawn lumber to build their shanties."

It was past midday when Mose finally drew his wagon to a creaking halt at the spot designated by Dave Salkeld. "This is it, Mose," said Dave, a gleam of enthusiasm in his eye. "What do you think of it?"

Mose looked over the big, diamond-shaped basin, with its far acres of grass, the sheltering, timbered ridges, the cold, foaming waters of the creek. His shining face became all one huge grin. "It's plumb scrumptious, Marse Dave." He beamed. "It sho' is. Ol' Mose can sho' be happy right here."

The adventurous, exciting part of the job was over with. Now came the toil. As soon as they had eaten the hasty meal Mose provided, Dave and his men headed for the timber slopes, axes tied to their saddles. The late afternoon and early twilight found the stand of virgin timber resounding to the first sound of ringing axes it had ever known.

For the next two days they toiled from dawn to dark. "First thing we got to do is build the cavvy corral," Dave had said.

And it was done. Long, arrow-straight poles from jack pine thickets were felled and trimmed and barked, then dragged down from the timber at the end of taut reatas. Thicker timbers for posts were cut and set and the spacious corral was built. That night Dave looked around the campfire and gave his orders. "Tonto and Pudge, you stay here with Mose. I don't know whether you'll have any trouble with settlers trying to edge in. You're liable to, for with the main basin filling up, they'll keep edging farther and farther out. If they do, you know our rights, Tonto. Be firm, but try and not make any enemies.

Remember, we're going to have to live along with these people for the rest of our lives. An enemy never rates as a profit in any man's book. Wampus, Dirk, Jumbo, and me . . . we head back for the Navajo River Meadows. Buck should be there with the herd when we arrive. Tonto, there's a pair of field glasses in the wagon. You keep watch on Antelope Pass. When you see the dust of the cattle coming through, you and Pudge head across the basin to help us."

They pulled out early the next morning, each man leading a relay of broncos, as they had on the way in. They struck the forks of the creek and turned down it a little way. Here, at regular intervals they found wagons and settlers, and in one particularly verdant-looking piece of bottom ground along the creek they struck the Abbott wagon.

A fire was burning beside the wagon and around it were grouped three people. Jim Abbott had his wounded arm in a rough sling, but he was looking much his old self again. He and Maidie greeted Dave and his riders cheerfully. But Lon Estes gave only a curt nod and kept his hard-faced, tight-lipped silence.

"Not leaving us, are you?" asked Abbott.

"Oh, no. Going out to bring in our herd. How's the arm?"

"Good enough. Thank that Tonto rider of yours for me. That balsam oil is great stuff."

"No more signs of trouble?"

Abbott frowned. "Not yet. That Tremper crowd have settled about three miles downstream. But they're keeping low. Good luck!"

Dave's last memory of the camp was a smile and a wave from the girl.

Their horses were still fresh and full of go when they reached Antelope Pass and they went through the savage wall well ahead of the blasting night winds. They rode the night out to strike Navajo River Meadows in the pale light of another dawn. There were still wagons toiling across the sage country beyond Vermilion Wall, and they passed the wreckage of many a wagon that would never roll again. At the Navajo River Meadows they found Buck Custer with the herd. Custer and Dave shook hands with real affection.

"Well, kid," asked the older man, "all set?"

Dave nodded. "All set, Buck. When did you get in with the herd?"

"Yesterday morning. The cattle have made the most of this grass and water and we can start over the rest of the drive any time."

"It is going to be tough traveling, from here to the Vermilion Wall," said Dave. "But we'll start this afternoon."

Dave and Jumbo and Dirk and Wampus got some sleep and by mid-afternoon the herd was across the river and under way. The six men that had helped Buck Custer bring the herd in from the old Stony Ford range were not Flying Diamond regulars. They were pick-up riders, but good men all. They, too, had felt the lure of a new frontier and had been glad to pay their way into Gallatin Basin by a riding job with the Flying Diamond herd. The agreement Custer had hired them under was that they would be paid off after the herd had reached its new range in Gallatin.

Throughout the balance of the day the herd moved steadily, riders at point, flank, and drag. Better than a day and night of rest and water and grazing along the Navajo River Meadows had put them in condition for another hard drive.

Behind the cattle traveled a cavvy herd of some forty saddle broncos and in back of all rolled another trail wagon, driven by a crooked-legged old cowpuncher, Frank Shore. Through the blue mystery of twilight and on into the starlit dark rumbled the herd, plodding out the slow miles of rolling sage country. In the dark, Vermilion Wall was only a dim, flat black line, seemingly marking the last rim of the world.

Midnight came and passed, with riders nodding sleepily in their saddles. But still the drive went on—went on to meet the ghostly, filtering dawn once more. As the world grew brighter, Dave Salkeld, riding at point, marked the distance they had come and nodded with satisfaction. The worst by far still lay ahead, but many valuable miles had been placed behind them.

The sun came up and the Vermilion Wall began to glow with its savage, warning color. As soon as the heat of the rising sun struck, the cattle began to lag. From now on the real work started.

It was hard on the men, hard on the horses, hardest on the cattle. The suffering brutes began their monotonous, bawling complaint for water. But there was no water. Only sandy earth and scrub sage and the burning, burning sun. Dust rose and hovered in a choking cloud, traveling tenaciously with the herd, making ghostly phantoms of cattle and riders alike.

Men tied neckerchiefs across mouth and nose and blinked through bloodshot, squinted eyes. But they kept a remorseless pressure on the herd and it went forward, forward, through the burning, ghastly hours of midday, through the searing afternoon. On and on, while the savage Vermilion Wall mocked them from the distance.

Weaker cattle began to drop out, despite all efforts to keep the exhausted brutes moving. When the riders saw that the case of the animal was hopeless, they drew guns and sent swiftly merciful bullets crashing home.

Nightfall found them still cursing the mocking distance of the wall. They bunched the herd and let it stop and bed down. The plaint for water was a continuous, never-ending bellow now—weaker than before. The wagon came up and a fire was started, and silent, haggard men ate and drank of the precious water in the keg on the wagon tailgate.

Dave and his partner compared notes. "We left just an even dozen back along the trail," said Custer. "That's better than I thought we'd do, Dave."

"We guessed fifty lost for the drive," said Dave. "That will be about right. When we hit that cussed pass tomorrow, they'll go fast, unless we reach it early. I suggest we take up the drive again, right after midnight."

"Suits me, if we can get the cattle up and moving."

Somehow they did it, after grabbing a few, all-too-short hours of rest themselves. It was like trying to stir some exhausted, insensate beast to movement, to get the herd once more on the trail, but once the start was made, the cattle plodded slowly on under the stars. The rest and the comparative coolness of the night, after the scorching sun, seemed to have given the herd new strength, and toward dawn the remnants of the wind that had poured through Antelope Pass reached them and invigorated them somewhat.

The rising sun found them but a few miles from the wall and the point riders were just entering the pass when the more hopeless cattle began going down again for the last time. Again came the single, flatly echoing shots of mercy. The frequency of them increased and the furnace walls of the pass rose and towered and blasted heat upon them.

That drive through Antelope Pass was to remain a nightmare to Dave Salkeld. The moan of the cattle lay along the walls like a voice of despair. Always there was that necessity of revolver work on downed cattle. Dave himself personally shot seven of the helpless creatures.

But there was no stopping now. The drive had to go through. And it did go through. Up at the point the first cooling breath of Gallatin Basin swept upward, carrying on it the magic lure of water—water. A new note came into the voices of the herd as scorched, dusty, and in some cases bloody nostrils scented that precious moisture.

The pace of the herd quickened. Most of the riders hurried up to point. The task of driving was over. The herd needed no urging now. The next task was to scatter the animals as they went down the far slope, so they would not mass and trample one another when they hit the creek waters beyond.

The terror of the pass was behind. Down the slope and into the timber poured the herd, crashing through jack pine thickets, floundering over deadfalls. And then the creek and the rushing water.

Riders spurred up and down the creek, yelling, cursing, swinging flailing rope ends, deliberately harrying the crazed brutes so they would not drink too much too quickly, and die of foundering. Yet another half dozen did die before the first thirst of the herd was quenched.

After that there was relaxation and rest and comparing of notes. "I make it forty-three lost, Dave," said Buck Custer, haggard, sunken-eyed but exultant.

"Forty-four," corrected Dave. "There's one down just above that big boulder yonder. Foundered. But we came through lucky, at that. Man . . . I'm glad that is over. We're here now, Buck. For better or for worse, we rise or fall with Gallatin Basin."

"Amen," said Buck.

CHAPTER NINE

Toward the fag end of the afternoon, Tonto and Pudge rode in. "By the look of things, you got some of the cattle through," said Pudge. "How many did you lose . . . about a hundred?"

"Hundred nothing," bawled Jumbo. "What do you think we are, a flock of tenderfeet? No, sir, we lost just forty-four, no more."

Tonto grinned and jabbed an elbow into Pudge's ribs. "Pay me," he said.

Pudge dug a dollar from his jeans and handed it over. "Tonto and me had a little bet. I said you'd lose close to a hundred, but Tonto said it wouldn't be over fifty. Anyhow, it's a bet I'm damned glad to pay."

"How are things on Cache Creek?" asked Dave.

"All right," Tonto answered. "A couple of wagons rolled in on our set-up, but when I explained matters to 'em, they moved out again."

"We don't want to have any trouble with the settlers," said Buck Custer.

"We're going to, though," said Tonto grimly. "Not from that angle, but in getting this herd across the basin to our range. Converse is in the basin with his herd. He came in around the north end of Vermilion Wall and he's moving the cattle right down through the heart of the basin. There are no fences up yet, of course, but the settlers are growing hostile. They're afraid of Converse. When they see cattle moving and grazing right over the new acres they've just settled on, they seem to see it as a permanent set-up. And they're scared. Converse, being the kind of arrogant, swaggering fool he is, ain't helping matters any. He got into a shooting scrape with a settler farther north and left the fellow crippled. The news of that fuss has spread and right now about every other settler you meet acts like there's nothing he'd like better than to lather the hide of every cattleman he sees with a load of buckshot. Just coming across the basin, Pudge and me got enough hostile looks to singe our hair. Eh, Pudge?"

"Damn' right. There was one old jigger forted up in his wagon, ready to blast us if we looked cross-eyed. We're going to have to do a lot of talking soft and talking tough to get through tomorrow."

They had a council of war around the fire that night. It was decided that Dave and Tonto should go out ahead and prepare the settlers along the route for the appearance of the herd. "Any danger of running into Converse's herd, Tonto?" asked Buck Custer.

"Not now. He's moved farther south. But he's left a bad flavor behind with the settlers and we're going to run into it."

"Well," said Buck philosophically, "no matter what we run into, it can't be any worse than the drive we've just covered."

Once more they were up in the first thin gray of dawn. By sunup they had the herd bunched and ready to go. Dave and Tonto spurred out ahead at a jog and were soon a couple of miles in advance. The first settler they ran into was a shock-headed, amiable Swede. He stood by his wagon, blinking at Dave and Tonto with mild, sea-blue eyes. Peeping from the wagon were two yellow-headed youngsters, while the Swede's wife, busy about her fire, smiled with shy pleasantry.

Dave explained quietly: "We're just moving the cattle through to our range on the far side of the basin, friend. We got 'em strung out so they won't trample any more of your grass than it's possible to prevent. We won't be bothering you any more and we expect to see the time when you'll be buying Flying Diamond beef to feed this fine family of yours."

The Swede nodded. It was all right with him. He was a peaceful man. He wanted no quarrel with anyone. Did they have time to take a cup of coffee?

Dave and Tonto drank the coffee with thanks, then, as they moved off, Dave spun a silver dollar into the wagon and grinned as he heard the scrambling and childish argument between the two little yellow heads.

"There's folks!" he exclaimed enthusiastically. "Now if all the settlers we meet are like that. . . ."

"They won't be," said Tonto grimly.

Tonto was right. They hit the first creek, which was dotted with wagons all along its winding length. As Dave and Tonto rode up, they were met by a lank, scowling fellow with a rifle across his arm.

"Ride wide, you saddle pounders," he growled. "We want no mix with any of your stripe. And don't try shooting up anybody along this creek, like you did that pore devil up north. You'll end up in hell, strung on a slug, if you do."

"None of our outfit was mixed up in that affair," said Dave. "Converse did that . . . Luke Converse and his crowd."

"Don't give a damn who did it," snapped the fellow stubbornly. "All you cow herders look alike to me. Ride wide . . . that's all."

From a camp across the creek two other men approached. They also carried weapons. They looked just as truculent and hostile as the first. Dave slouched sideways in his saddle, building a cigarette.

"Let's talk sense," he said quietly. "There is a herd coming up behind me and my partner here. We're aiming for our new range over in the foothills of the Windy Mountains. Once we get there, we stay there. We want no quarrel with you settlers. We don't want any of this bottom land for range. We got plenty of it in the foothills. The herd won't be over half an hour in passing. That will be the last you'll see of it. There ain't a thing we can harm."

The first settler shook a stubborn head. "No go. First damned cow that sets a foot on my property gets a dose of lead."

Dave's eyes narrowed, grew chill. "You other *hombres* feel the same way about it?"

They nodded. "We shore as hell do."

"All right," snapped Dave. "While you're waiting for the herd to get here, you might as well take picks and shovels and begin digging your own graves. For you'll end up in them. There are plenty of men coming along with that herd. They brought it clear from Stony Ford. They brought it across the Navajo River. They brought it over that desert stretch the other side Vermilion Wall. And they brought it through that hell-blasted Antelope Pass. After all that, if you think they're going to be stopped by three lunkheads like you . . . then you are loco." He turned to Tonto and gave an imperceptible wink. "Drift on back to the herd, Tonto. Tell Buck to send half a dozen of the boys up ahead with Winchesters. Tell him we got three damned fools here who want to die."

"OK, Dave," said Tonto, starting to swing his horse. One of the settlers made a move with his rifle, only to find himself staring into the round, blue eye of Dave's gun. "Drop it!" crackled Dave.

The settler gulped, and dropped his weapon.

One of the others spoke: "Wait a minute . . . wait a minute. Ain't no use running this thing into a shoot-out. You mean it, cowboy . . . when you say you're taking those cattle over into the foothills of the Windies?"

"I said so, didn't I?" growled Dave. "The north fork of Cache Creek, to be exact. You, or no other settler in this basin, has got a thing to fear from the Flying Diamond outfit. I can't vouch for Luke Converse and his crowd. But I can speak for the Flying Diamond. Once we get our herd onto that foothill range, we stay there and mind our own business."

"All right. Move your cattle through."

Dave and Tonto rode on.

Tonto chuckled. "When you turned tough, you fooled even me for a minute, Dave."

Dave's face was grim. "Bluffs are made to be called. Just the same, those fools would have got a working over if they hadn't seen the light."

All the way across the basin it was the same. A few of the settlers were fair, friendly folk, like the first one Dave and Tonto had encountered. But most were surly, suspicious, inclined to be hostile. Dave used persuasion, argument, and, when these did not work, direct threat. And the threat worked, for the settlers were still unorganized and no individual wanted to dare the wrath of a well-organized cattle outfit.

Dave's patience was worn pretty thin by the time they struck Cache Creek. "If I had to coddle any more of those thick-headed damn' fools, I'd start gun-whipping some sense into them," he snarled. "Thank God that's over with."

They turned in their saddles and looked back, from the eminence of the first rise of the foothill country. Out there behind them, winding across the basin, was a long cloud of dust. Sight of it calmed Dave's taut nerves. That long file of cattle was just another part of this great hegira into a new land, a new frontier. It was a monument to his part in the establishing of another frontier empire. A warm, stirring exaltation ran through him.

For the next two weeks Dave Salkeld did not leave the limits of the north fork valley range. Instead of paying off the riders who had helped Buck Custer make the drive in from Stony Ford, Dave and Buck decided to keep them on for a time, using them to help build the new headquarters.

There was no need to watch the cattle any more. Here in this verdant valley, fed by the rushing creek, the cattle grazed and rested and grew fat once more. From dawn to dark the timber slopes echoed to the ring of axes, to the crash of falling timbers, and the whine of cross-cut saws.

Logs were snaked down, peeled, shaped, and skidded into place. Walls grew, pole rafters went into place, and roofs set down of shakes, split from billets of straight-grained, rich-smelling cedar. Feed sheds, bunkhouse, barns took form, low and stout and sturdy. A tangle of corrals took on a pattern. Mose labored and sang happily in a cook shack, the new long walls of which oozed drops of pungent resin.

Then one day Buck Custer drew Dave aside. "We can't afford to hole up here forever and not know what is developing down in the basin," said Buck. "You better take a ride in to Boardman's Flat, kid, and sort of take a look-see. But don't go alone. Take somebody with you."

Dave was more than willing. He had been growing restless. He was wondering about many things—the Abbots, that Tremper crowd, and Converse. He had wondered a lot about Converse. A wise man kept an eye on the movement of a potential enemy. So, with Jumbo beside him, Dave rode down to the, basin.

At the Abbott claim there was Jim Abbott, plodding behind his team, his plow turning up a deep, black furrow of virgin, rich sod. Abbott reined in, leaned against his plow handles. "Hello, boys," he greeted. "How are things up on the north fork?"

"Good enough, Jim," answered Dave. "How's the shoulder?"

Abbott flexed it. "Never better. Heading for Boardman's?"

"Yeah. Anything you want brought out?"

"Maybe. You can ask Maidie. She's at the wagon." Abbott scrubbed his chin soberly. "Watch yourself in town, Dave."

"Why?"

"You're cowmen. And cowmen are growing plenty unpopular in Gallatin Basin."

"Converse?"

"Converse. He's raised hell and put a rock under it. He and his outfit got into a shooting fest down at the southern end of the basin with some settlers. Converse got the worst of it. He lost two riders. One settler was killed and two others wounded. The word has traveled. Right now a man in chaps and spurs is like a red flag to some of the settlers. So . . . watch yourselves."

"Thanks, Jim. We will."

As Dave and Jumbo came up to the Abbott wagon, Maidie Abbott stepped around to meet them. There was a tenseness in the tilt of her head and the tautness of her slim shoulders. Beside her was Lon Estes, arguing something in a low tone.

Maidie paid him no attention, throwing up a hand in welcome as she hurried forward to meet Dave. Estes stopped at the end of the wagon, lithe and still and queerly hostile.

"Dave Salkeld!" exclaimed Maidie. "I am glad to see you. Where have you been keeping yourself?"

Her eyes were suspiciously bright, as though anger had touched them recently. An angry color glowed in her cheeks.

"Been working like all get out, building our headquarters," said Dave. "Your dad said there might be something we could bring you from town."

Her lips tightened. "If you could take me to town with you, I'd appreciate that most," she said fiercely.

Dave grinned. "We could do that, too. You can have my bronc' and I'll double up with Jumbo."

She laughed. "Forget it. I was just fooling. You can bring us a side of bacon and a can of baking powder."

"Sure." Dave nodded. "Make a note of that, Jumbo." He looked straight into her troubled eyes. "Gets a little tiresome, I suspect, staying right here all the time."

She nodded soberly. "But . . . forget it," she said again. "I guess I'm just a restless, flighty creature."

"A mighty pretty one," murmured Dave softly. "And you've given me an idea. We'll bring that grub for you."

As they rode past the wagon, Dave nodded. "Hello, Estes," he said.

The answering nod was barely perceptible. There was no spoken answer. Estes's face was a tight, hard mask, his eyes blank and hostile.

Dave Salkeld was amazed at the change in Boardman's Flat in the space of two short weeks. Sprawling, uncouth, ugly, it was a roaring, unruly town. Walls of new yellow timber were going up everywhere, hammers *clanging*, saws *whining*. The town was a hive of people of all sorts.

Dave and Jumbo found a place for their broncos beside a battered settler's wagon. As they dismounted, a snarling voice reached them. "Damned thievin' saddle pounders!"

A bearded, hostile-eyed settler was on the wagon seat, scowling at them. Jumbo, a growl of truculence in his throat, started to turn, but Dave caught him by the arm.

"Easy," murmured Dave. "Words won't hurt you. We got to get used to this. They'll know better in time. Come on, you big hot-headed ape . . . come on."

Dave led the still grumbling Jumbo into Boardman's. It was a hive of activity. Bill Boardman, sweating profusely, still with that dazed, wild-eyed look, was rushing here and there, trying to wait on a dozen customers at once. He bumped into Dave and answered the latter's greeting with a sort of numb nod. "How're you?" he gulped. "Got no time now. Nuts . . . crazy . . . the whole world's gone bughouse. They won't let me alone. Can't hardly sleep nights. Ruinin' my health. All nuts, I tell you."

Somebody yelled for him and he rushed away. Jumbo laughed. "There's a guy gettin' rich and goin' half loco gettin' there. I can't feel sorry for him."

"We'll come back later," said Dave. "Let's look around."

They went out into the clamoring street again. Whenever they met a settler, they met savage, hostile looks. It began to get under even Dave's hide. Jumbo was seething at some of the remarks thrown their way. "In just about a minute," he fumed, "I'm going to knock the teeth out of one of these lunkheaded sodbusters. There's a limit to what a man can stand."

A hulking settler of about Dave's age faced them. "Lousy saddle pounders," he reviled. "I shore hate your dirty hides." Then he spat and added an unforgivable epithet.

Dave's self-control snapped. He laid all his strength into a right-hand smash that caught the fellow fully in his foul mouth, knocking him down. A yell went up and a crowd of settlers jammed about them. "Get the damned leather pants!" yelled someone. "Let's show 'em who's runnin' this basin."

"Back to back, Jumbo!" snapped Dave. "Throw down on the fools. If they insist on it, give it to 'em. I'm sick of this rawhidin'. I thought we could dodge it, but it looks like we can't."

At sight of ready guns, the crowd gave back, snarling and cursing. One lank fellow, who loomed head and shoulders above the rest, bawled recklessly: "Rush 'em! Rush 'em! Grab those guns and choke 'em with 'em."

Dave's gun leaped in recoil and bellowed a flat report. The lanky one's hat lifted, half turned, and settled back over one eye. The owner of it gulped and ran for shelter. "The next one goes center if you try and rush us," crackled Dave. "Break it up!"

The crowd broke and Dave and Jumbo gained the shelter of the trading post again. Jumbo was mumbling wrathfully. Dave's face was all lean, cold angles. Boardman grabbed Dave's arm. "Just heard a shot. Who got it this time?"

"Nobody," rapped Dave. "Just a fool settler who got a little air into his hat to cool his crazy brains. I want a side of bacon and a can of baking powder."

Carrying his purchases, Dave stalked out to his horse. He looked across his saddle at Jumbo. "We can thank Converse for this sort of trouble, of course," he growled. "It's going to be Converse or us, one of these days, Jumbo. This basin ain't big enough to hold his outfit and ours at the same time. Come on."

As they left town, they passed Lon Estes, riding hard. The gunman gave no sign that he had seen them at all.

CHAPTER TEN

Maidie Abbott was washing clothes. Half a line of laundry was already fluttering on a line strung between two handy cottonwoods, and she still had half a tub more to go. She was scrubbing away when she heard the sound of hoofs and looked around to see Dave Salkeld just riding in, leading behind him a saddled but riderless horse.

Maidie felt a little confused as Dave drew to a halt and grinned down at her. She was prettier than he dreamed, with her cheeks pink from exertion, her fair curly hair shining in the sun.

"You should have given me warning, sir," she scolded ruefully. "Don't you know you should never surprise a lady busy at a laundry tub? She always looks her worst at such a time . . . and knows it."

Dave's grin became a chuckle. "And here I was thinking what a pretty picture you made. Don't apologize, please."

She wiped her hands on her gingham apron and pushed stray locks back from her face. "Dad's gone over to that new sawmill to dicker for some lumber for a cabin. And am I glad! I don't mind a wagon to travel in, but when I set up permanent housekeeping, I admit I prefer a house of some kind. Where are you taking that horse?"

"Here," said Dave, dismounting and placing the rein in Maidie's startled hand. "Yours. With the compliments of the Flying Diamond outfit."

Maidie gasped: "Mine? You mean . . . this horse and saddle are . . . mine?"

"That's right." Dave smiled. "Mose sent the saddle and the rest of us threw in the mare. Now when you get restless, you can get up and, as Mose put it, fly like a li'l bird."

She looked at him, her eyes wide and dazed. Swift color came and went in her cheeks. "Oh . . . but I can't. I can't take such a valuable present. You've got to take it back, Dave."

Dave built a cigarette. "Nothing doing. I brought the bronc' down here. I'm not taking it back. And all that talk about a valuable present doesn't mean a thing. Shucks! The mare is no good. Just an ugly little scrub, slow as molasses, knot-headed, spavined, and full of ring bones. The saddle is all rat-eaten and. . . ."

"That isn't so!" cried Maidie. "The mare is a gorgeous little thing. And the saddle is almost new. I'll have you understand I know a little about such things."

Then she saw the teasing twinkle in Dave's eyes, and laughed breathlessly. "Of course you were fooling. But seriously, though I'd love to accept, I can't. Thanks so much, just the same."

Dave sighed dolefully. "I knew you were going to be a stubborn little wench. Now look. Mose gave you the saddle. The black rascal has got so fat he can't get into it any more. If he thought you'd turned his present down, it would break his heart. The mare is one of my string. But she's too light to stand up under the pounding of cattle work. If you don't take her, it is only a matter of time before she gets so stove up I'll have to shoot her. And you wouldn't want that, would you?"

Maidie looked at him with dancing eyes, then laughed merrily. "I see I might as well accept. But you don't get off scotfree, sir. You must do penance. You've got to take me for a ride, just as soon as I finish this tub of clothes."

Dave squatted on his heels, watching her. He thought that he had never seen such a completely wholesome little person as Maidie Abbott. Her face was firm without being hard. She was slim and graceful and strong. She had a trick of pushing out her red lower lip and blowing aside strands of hair that fell over her face. It was an elfin, entirely delightful expression. She soon finished with her washing, and then ran for the wagon. "I'll be only a jiffy!" she cried.

When she did appear, Dave was amazed. He had expected her to emerge in the overalls and hickory shirt attire she had been wearing when he first laid eyes on her. But this slim figure in divided skirt of corduroy, woolen blouse, and trim little boots was completely feminine and charming. She laughed at Dave's surprise.

"Oh, I've been on a horse before, cowboy. Back home I rode a lot. And now I want to ride up into the timber." Maidie tossed her fair head. "I don't care. Let 'em stare and mumble and snuffle to themselves. My life is my own . . . and my friends."

"Then I'm a friend of yours?"

Her cheeks pinked swiftly as she looked away. "I'm riding your gift horse, am I not? Oh . . . look, Dave . . . there goes a deer!"

It was that way all along the ride. Maidie's quick eye picked up the slightest movement of the teeming wildlife, and each glimpse seemed to fill her with quick joy.

In time they topped a ridge where the timber thinned and they could look across and down into a wide, park-like basin where the timber ran out again into grassland. In the middle of the wide expanse of grass country was a timber island. Dave pointed.

"More of our range," he said. "We'll use it for summer grazing. Looks like a few of our cattle have already found their way up here. Yonder, in that timber island, is a spring. We're going to build a line camp cabin there. And later on. . . ."

He broke off, listening—stiffened and alert in his saddle. Echoing up through the timber came the rumble of a shot. Maidie looked at Dave with wide eyes. "What . . . what is it?"

"Don't know," said Dave, his eyes narrowing. "Maybe a settler getting a piece of venison. Maybe one of our boys. But that isn't likely. Wampus brought in a deer just a couple of days ago. I think I'll go down and investigate. You stay here."

"I will not! I'm going with you."

Dave hesitated, then nodded. "All right. Let me go ahead. And keep quiet."

Dave let his bronco down through the timber with expert judgment, avoiding downed timber, keeping his mount to the deep, soft carpet of pine needles in which the animal's hoofs sank with hardly any sound. Maidie followed him, her wide eyes on the grimly intent silhouette of Dave Salkeld's head and shoulders. She liked the picture. He had a lean, rather splendid head, and his profile was that of clean-cut strength, tempered with a judgment beyond his years. She got the impression now that he heard every sound, saw every movement.

Several hundred yards they wended that cautious, quiet way. Then Maidie noticed a restlessness begin to show in both her own and Dave's mounts. The horses seemed to be sniffing the air. Then the little mare let out a gusty snort.

From the timber below them someone shouted a warning. Down through the shadowy aisles of the timber, beyond a fringe of scrub jack pine, there was a flurry of motion, of men and horses. A gun snarled, once—twice. A gout of bark fragments leaped from the bole of a towering sugar pine, not two feet from Maidie's head. Where the speeding slug had struck, a ragged tear of white wood showed.

Dave Salkeld had a gun out now and was shooting in return, chopping down at the fleeing figures of mounted men. One of those flitting figures turned in his saddle and flung a final shot.

Dave's horse shivered all over and dropped in its tracks, shot through the head.

Then those flitting figures were gone, the sound of their progress a fading crashing. Dave, lunging free of his fallen mount, whirled on Maidie. His gray eyes were blazing with a cold fire. "Give me that bronc'!" he rasped. "I'll show those dirty rats!"

"No!" cried Maidie. "No, Dave! You stay here! There were three or four of them. You could not catch them, anyhow!"

For a moment she thought he was going to jerk her from the saddle. Little cavities of white quivered at the corners of his taut lips. Then, of a sudden, he relaxed.

"You're right," he said. "They can wait."

"Who were they? What were they doing here?"

"Some of the Tremper gang. We'll take a look at what they were doing. Come on."

They went down the slope beyond the jack pines. Maidie had dismounted and led the nervous, snorting little mare behind her.

"Thought so," growled Dave. "They were slow-elking."

There, under the timber, lay the body of a steer. It had been shot through the head with a rifle bullet. It had been bled and dressed and was half skinned out. Dave lifted a loose flap of the skin, turned it over, and pointed. On the skin, clear and sharp from a stamp iron, showed a Flying Diamond brand.

"One of ours," said Dave. "A prime three-year-old."

"B-but they could have gotten a deer if they wanted fresh meat. Why . . . ?"

"Because fresh beef ought to bring a pretty good price down among those settlers in the basin. Listen, here is what you do, Maidie. Cut right on down through this timber. Soon as you get out in the grass country, swing north. You'll be able to see the top of Painted Rock. Right down below Painted Rock is our headquarters. There's a trail down just this side of the rock. You tell Buck Custer what happened. Have him send a couple of the boys up here with some pack horses and a spare bronc' for me. The outfit will eat this meat. You wait down there with Mose. I'll take you home, later."

She looked at him steadily, then nodded. "All right, Dave. I . . . I don't suppose those no-accounts will try and come back before your riders get here?"

His face was still grim, but he smiled at her. "I'll be all right. You cut along, like a good youngster. See you later."

She swung into the saddle and reined off down through the timber, a slim, gallant little figure. Dave watched her out of sight, his eyes musing, growing softer. Then, as she vanished, he pulled a pocket knife, opened it, and got to work on the dead steer.

Dave had the steer completely skinned out and was quartering it, a pretty tough job with only a pocket knife, when he heard Jumbo's hoarse bellow down at the fringe of timber. Dave answered, and soon up through the trees came Buck Custer, Jumbo, and Tonto, leading horses behind them.

"That Abbott girl said it was the Tremper gang," rapped Buck. "Right, Dave?"

Dave nodded. "Right. Four of them. We swapped some lead. They got my horse. This is one of our prize three-year-olds, Buck. In a way, this slow-elking try doesn't surprise me any. There are a lot of folks down in the basin who'll pay good money for fresh beef, and not give a damn whether it's slow-elked or not."

"But they don't get away with it," rumbled Jumbo.

"No," said Dave. "They don't get away with it. We're making a little call on the Tremper crowd this afternoon. This ain't what you'd call a high-class job of butchering, but it's the best I could do with just a pocket knife. You fellows can load up this meat while I go up and get my saddle."

It was just after 1:00 p.m. as they filed down the Painted Rock trail and on across the valley to headquarters. They brought the meat up to the cook shack, where Maidie Abbott and Mose stood waiting.

"We'll take no excuses for not living high from now on, Mose," said Dave with a grim smile. "Look what we brought you."

"Those rapscallions," snorted Mose. "They no-good white trash, those Trempers. They better leave our cattle plumb alone, 'fore ole Mose take after 'em with the cleaver. Lawdy, Marse Dave . . . this yere an awful lot of meat. Reckon most of it'll have to be salted down. Consarn those no-good Trempers, anyhow. Come along and eat, now. Yo' dinner's plumb spillin' on the table."

Maidie sat between Dave and Buck Custer. Wampus and Dirk and Pudge and the other riders had to hear the story. Mose, shuffling back and forth from stove to table, mumbled and growled to himself about the "no-account, white trash Trempers."

"Best thing we can do is get that line camp cabin built as soon as possible and keep at least one man up there all the time," said Buck Custer. "The cattle just naturally are going to drift up into that basin, and there's no reason why they shouldn't. But we got to keep an eye on them."

Dave nodded. "We start building that cabin tomorrow."

There was no talk of what was going to be done that afternoon, but Maidie, watching the grave faces about the table, knew that these were not the kind of men to take what the Trempers had started, without having plenty to say about it. So she was not surprised when, after the meal, Dave and Buck,

Tonto and Jumbo strapped saddle guns to their riding rigs before swinging astride.

"Come along." Dave smiled. "But you'll have to visit us again when I'll have time to show you around."

Maidie ran into the cook shack and pressed one of Mose's big fists. "Thanks so much for that saddle, Mose," she told him breathlessly. "It was mighty sweet of you."

Mose beamed all over. "Bless yo' li'l heart, honey . . . if it make yo' happy, then it make ole Mose jest twice as happy. It shore do."

Maidie's eyes were a little misty as she swung into that saddle. She saw Dave watching her. "Mose," she said a little unsteadily, "is pure gold."

Dave nodded. "He'll do. He rates aces with this outfit. The boys would fight a buzz saw for Mose."

At the Abbott wagon they found Jim Abbott and Lon Estes. Abbott hailed them with relief. "You had me worried," he told Maidie, his voice gruff, but his eyes fond. "Where you been, lass?"

"Riding through all kinds of adventures," explained Maidie happily. "Look, Dad . . . my saddle, my pony. Gifts from the Flying Diamond outfit."

"Sa-ay," exclaimed Abbott, "that is something! Pretty handsome of the Flying Diamond."

"You don't mind if I keep them?" asked Maidie anxiously.

"Of course he don't," said Buck Custer, smiling. "But we're going to claim a price. You got to ride up and visit us real often."

"Oh, I'll do that all right." Maidie laughed. "Dad, their cook, Mose, makes the most heavenly dried-apple pies."

Abbott chuckled, then eyed the saddle guns Dave and the others carried. "You look like you might be going on a hunt of some sort," he said shrewdly.

103

"Coyotes." Dave nodded briefly. "Well, boys . . . let's drift. See you folks later." He looked straight at Maidie. "Thanks for riding with me." He smiled down into her eyes, then reined away.

Maidie watched them go anxiously.

"Who are they after, lass?" asked her father.

"The Trempers. Dave and I . . . we rode over through that far stretch of timber. We were on the backbone when we heard a shot, down in the timber on the far side. We rode down there and surprised the Trempers, slow-elking a Flying Diamond beef. They shot at us and killed Dave's horse. Now . . . now I guess they're going to wish they hadn't."

"Those Trempers," growled Abbott. "All they do is make trouble. They ought to be run out of the basin. Well, I promised Sam Olson I'd help him get a load of lumber this afternoon. I got to be going. It will be dark, I expect, lass, before I get back."

Abbott hurried away. Left to her thoughts, Maidie unsaddled her mare, gave the sleek little animal a good rub-down with a piece of burlap, watered her, then picketed her out in the meadow. When she returned to the wagon, Lon Estes was standing there, waiting for her. His thin face was bleak, his eyes harsh.

Chapter Eleven

When Maidie Abbott had laid eyes on Lon Estes for the first time in her life, her only feeling had been one of pity, natural pity for a fellow human lying wounded and exhausted beside a chance trail. All through the time her father and herself had nursed him back to strength, that pity had continued. But as the man grew stronger, became more his real self, Maidie had sensed dark undercurrents in Estes that at first repelled her, then made her uneasy and fearful. Now, as she faced him, that fear grew very swiftly. The man looked savage as a wolf.

His voice bit at her harshly: "Going soft on that Salkeld *hombre*, eh?"

Maidie flushed, meeting the moiling darkness of his eyes with erect head. "Dave Salkeld has been very nice to me," she countered. "Either way, it is my affair."

"And mine," rapped Estes flatly. "I won't stand for it."

The color in Maidie's face took on the deeper tone of rising anger. "Lon," she said in an ominously quiet tone, "I don't want to quarrel with you. I told you that before when you've questioned me about . . . about Dave Salkeld. Now please . . . you're only making things unpleasant for both of us."

Estes built a cigarette with jerky, yet deft movements of hands and fingers. He inhaled deeply, marched back and forth with short, choppy strides. His dark, thin face was working queerly.

"You don't understand," he said hoarsely. "I'm making no attempt to cover up the years before I met you, Maidie Abbott.

105

I'm not excusing them, though I was more or less kicked into life and had to claw my way through the pack to keep alive. I never knew my mother. My father was an outlaw who rode with one of the wildest gangs ever to hit the West. I was raised among those outlaws. As a kid I never knew anything but violence and savagery and brutality. It warped me . . . it was bound to. My father taught me all he knew about throwing a gun, and he knew plenty. And one day, right before my eyes, he was ganged by three other outlaws and shot down. I got the three who got him." He took another heavy drag of the cigarette, then tossed it aside, his fingers snapping. "That was the way it started," he went on thinly. "I've rode as wild as any man who ever drew breath. What I wanted out of life, I took. I could see no good in any mortal man, woman, or child. And then I met you. And I knew I'd been wrong . . . all wrong. Knowing you lifted me out of the shadows . . . and I mean to stay out. Even if I have to kill Dave Salkeld to stay out."

It was the first time Estes had told Maidie anything like this. It moved her strangely until he made that final threat—that he would kill Dave Salkeld if the mood struck him so. That quickened Maidie's anger again.

"I don't like that talk, Lon," she said crisply. "I can sympathize with your past misfortunes and feel sorry for you because of them. Oh, I know what is in your mind. I know that you came on ahead of the wagon, settled this spot of ground for us, then signed it over to Dad. I know that you killed one of the Trempers for trying to knife Dad. Had you done those things in pure generosity, through a spirit of unselfish friendship, I could admire you. As it is, you force me to remind you of something. On that long drive in from home to the Navajo River Meadows, Dad and I found you beside the trail, badly wounded. You probably would have lived, anyhow, if we had not found you. Yet the main fact is that we did find you, that we picked you up, took care of you. and nursed you back to quick health. Neither Dad nor I asked or expected any reward for that act of simple human kindness. It was you who suggested you come in ahead and make sure of this piece of ground for us. So it seems to me that the debt is pretty even and we can write off all favors as strictly balanced."

"To hell with favors, back and forth," spat Estes. "I'm not thinking about any damn' favors. I'm thinking about you . . . and me. I'm trying to tell you that I never cared a snap of a finger for any woman until I met you. Call it the only decent thing that ever happened to me, if you want. The only decent thing in a lifetime of hell. You're the lone glimpse of heaven I ever had. I mean to hang on to that glimpse."

Maidie knew he meant what he said. In this lithe, thin-faced gunman with the old, hard eyes there burned a strange, dark passion for her. For so long she had sensed this fact, and had tried to put it aside, for it made her uncomfortable. But now she had to face it. This man, she knew, would cheerfully die for her. Yet. . . .

"Listen, Lon," she said, almost gently. "You still don't understand. I could go on liking you as a friend. But beyond that. . . ."

He made a short, fierce gesture and into his voice came an explosive emotion. "You could learn to care for me. Everything that has gone before, I can put aside. I can make a new start in a new world. I can hang up my guns . . . for good. You're the one person in this world I'd do that for."

Maidie shook her head slowly. "No, Lon . . . you couldn't do that. You might think so now. But at some future time, on provocation, you'd go right back to the old ways. Even so, if I cared for you that way, I'd go to the end of the world with you and take my chances. But I don't care that way, Lon . . . and I never could. Don't you understand?"

He came closer to her and there burned in his eyes a flame
that made Maidie take an involuntary backward step. She was
very sure of everything now. This man could never change,
never really learn to govern himself. In him there flowed dark,
malignant currents, ever at cross-purposes with one another.
Always he would be like some partially tamed panther, submit-
ting to a caressing hand one moment, the next striking out with
savage, unruly wild claws. No, he could never change. As for
herself, while she might fear him, it was inconceivable that she
could ever love him. No—never that.

"You're the one who doesn't understand," he said hoarsely.
"I'm putting in your hands the life and future of a man.
Somehow I know that right now I'm at the final forks of the
trail. A word from you can put me on the right trail . . . or the
wrong one. There'll be no turning back again, once I start.
Don't forget that."

Maidie could not keep the contempt out of her voice. " 'Way
down deep I know you pride yourself on being a man of
strength, a man of courage. Yet, Lon Estes, you'd try and force
me to a decision against all my feelings and judgment with such
a cowardly plea as that. If you were half a man, you'd recognize
the right trail and take it without any urging from me. Or
sacrifice on my part, either. Now you're becoming contempt-
ible."

She knew that her words were scarring the turgid soul of him
like lashes from a whip. She could see his face twist and writhe.
"Listen," he rasped thickly. "Get this straight, once and for all.
If you don't marry me, you'll never marry any man. Because I'll
kill any man who tries to take you away from me. I'll kill him . . .
understand! And I don't care who he is."

Maidie's contempt became flaming anger. "That's enough!"
she cried. "I don't care to hear any more of that kind of talk.
Right now I'm not concerned with marrying any man. There is

only one person I love, and that is my father. But if I ever do fall in love, I'll marry. And I'll defend the man I marry, if I have to shoot you myself. You talk of caring for me, of loving me. Why, you don't know the meaning of the word. True love is unselfish. And this feeling you have is just black, dirty selfishness. If you really cared for me, you'd want me to be happy. But no . . . you threaten and bully me. You tell me you'd shoot any man I happened to fall in love with. Why, you're not a man, you're just a black, bitter animal. I think it would be very wise if you left this camp . . . and never came back!"

There was something rather magnificent about Maidie Abbott at that moment, as she flayed Lon Estes with righteous scorn and contempt. Her cheeks were flaming, her eyes flashing, her head high and unafraid.

Estes stared at her a little stupidly, as though he could hardly realize the final import of her words. Then his face became so bleak and drawn, it seemed as if the bones were going to split the skin. His hands opened and closed, quivering and shaking like dangling talons. A thin, cold laugh ripped from his lips and his eyes became mocking, turgid black pools.

"Keno," he hissed. "That ends it. Hell I was born to, hell is where I'll travel. Remember that."

He whirled, almost ran to his horse, saddling the startled brute with swift, jerky motions. He leaped into the saddle, and with viciously cruel spurs drove the horse ahead in several long leaps, bringing it close to the little mare that was grazing so quietly in the meadow. Then, all in one flashing move, he drew a gun and shot the mare squarely through the head. Estes whirled back toward the stunned and broken-hearted girl.

"There it is!" he yelled. "That's my answer to you and Salkeld! And the next slug goes for him in the same place!"

Then he was gone in a wild gallop, spurring his frantic,

squealing mount savagely.

The Tremper camp was on Cache Creek, some distance below the Abbott section. From behind a screen of willows, Dave Salkeld and his men looked over that renegade camp. A group of horses were picketed near the wagon, while old Zeph Tremper and his remaining sons were squatting in the shade of the wagon, engrossed in some kind of an argument or council of war.

"A rope is what that worthless bunch should get," Dave growled. "But we got to remember they're settlers, and, should we string 'em up, we'd have a flock of other settlers down our necks. Tonto, you and Jumbo cut downcreek and come up on them from the other side. Buck and I go in from here. We'll give you ten minutes. Travel."

Tonto and Jumbo spurred away, keeping the brush lining the creek between them and the Tremper camp. Buck looked at his younger partner. "What do you aim to do, Dave?"

"Start 'em traveling somewhere. Run 'em down to the southern end of the basin, probably. They're too close to our range here. We get 'em well away from us, we'll have less trouble in the future."

At the end of ten minutes, Dave settled himself a little more firmly in the saddle, then spurred into the open, riding straight for the Tremper wagon. He and Buck were hardly clear of the brush before they were seen. There was a blur of activity about the wagon, and then they heard the thin harshness of Zeph Tremper's voice snarling at his sons. They gathered in a group about the old man, sullen and defiant, watching Dave and Buck approach.

Twenty feet from them, Dave reined in. He saw that there were several weapons within easy reach. "Let me do the talking, Buck," he murmured. "You watch 'em. If any of 'em makes a grab for a gun, let 'em have it."

"We're waitin'," snarled Zeph Tremper. "Whatever is on your minds, best shuck it and get travelin'. We want no truck with any of you damned leather pants."

"So-o," drawled Dave, "too bad you don't feel the same about our cattle, Tremper."

"Cattle? I don't know what you mean."

"Oh, yes, you do. Don't waste your breath lying. You know why we're here. Tremper, there are several things the Flying Diamond doesn't stand for. One is slow-elking of our cattle."

"Yeah? Well, what's that got to do with me and my boys?"

Dave stared at him coldly. "No wonder you got a rattlesnake brood. They don't come any crookeder and full of lying worthlessness than you. I won't mince words. This morning I ran across your darling sons slow-elking a Flying Diamond three-year-old. I caught 'em in the act. My eyes are good. I know what I see. Your lies won't get you clear."

Zeph Tremper looked like a lank, venomous, deadly old spider. His lips were twisted to show broken, stained teeth. "That's what you say," he spat. "My boys ain't been over fifty yards from this wagon all day. Their word against yours . . . and see what you can do about it."

"I know what I'm going to do about it," said Dave. "I don't intend to argue with you any longer. I'm just going to tell you what to do. You and your breed are just plain no good, Tremper. Back at the camp along the Navajo River you made trouble. One of you tried to throw a knife into me because I helped Jim Abbott in that row you started over the use of the forge. Then at the wagon camp across Vermilion Wall, one of you tried to knife Jim Abbott in the night. Lon Estes evened up for that. Whether he got the right man or not, I don't know. But he took care of one of you. Now we find you slow-elking Flying Diamond cattle. Do you think we're fools enough to let you get away with that? Hardly. So here's what you're going to have to do. It just isn't possible for you to act decent and get along with the folks about you. Crooked knife work, thieving, and all other brands of cussedness run out of you like water out of a jug. You and your crowd are just plain undesirables. So we do what anyone else would do under the same set-up. We're inviting you to move on."

"Move on! What do you mean, move on?"

"Just that. Load your wagon and get the hell out!"

"And leave this section of free land we've settled on! You're loco. We won't do it. We stay right here, which we're entitled to, same as any other settler."

"You'll never do this ground any good. You'll only sour it. You're leaving, Tremper. Start packing."

Zeph Tremper stared for a moment, then spat savagely. "What authority you got to try and make us move?" he yelled. "What . . . ?"

Dave patted his gun butts. "This authority, Tremper. I'm all through arguing. Start packing!"

A snarl ran through the four Tremper boys. "Say the word, Pap. We'll give these two leather pants all the gun argument they want," growled one of them.

"Before you try," barked Dave crisply, "I'd suggest you look behind you."

They did look, and saw Tonto and Jumbo coming up in back of them. For a moment they were disconcerted, uncertain. Dave seized the moment. He flashed his guns. "Drop your guns . . . out in the open. Quick!"

The Trempers did not have the courage for this sort of thing, out in the open, man to man. Their forte was knife work, in the dark if possible. Or bushwhacking from some covert, when the odds were all with them. But there were no odds here, only four grim cowboys, watching their every move with the alertness of hawks. One by one the Trempers stepped out, piled their weapons on the ground.

"That's better," rapped Dave. "Now get busy."

They harnessed a team and hitched it to the wagon. They saddled other broncos. Old man Tremper, cursing venomously all the while, threw equipment into the wagon.

"We'll be back," he blustered. "You can't treat good honest settlers like this and get away with it. You'll find out you're not running this basin. Yeah, we'll be back, and, when we get you with the odds the other way, you'll sing a damned different song."

"Shut up!" said Dave crisply. "And get going."

Zeph Tremper climbed up on to the wagon box. There was a red, growing rage in his mean little eyes. Without a word of warning he reached back into the wagon, snatched a hidden gun, and threw down on Dave.

Dave had been watching the other Trempers, and the old man's move would have caught him cold. But not so the wary old Tonto, over on the other side of the wagon. Tonto made a lightning draw. The crash of his gun, and that of the one Zeph Tremper had, sounded almost together. Invisible fingers jerked at a fold of Dave's shirt.

Zeph Tremper reeled and fell from the wagon, and he flopped around on the ground, yelling and cursing with a smashed shoulder. The three Tremper boys, having just mounted, spun their broncos, raging.

"You dirty whelps!" yelled one of them. "You pulled a sneak play on the old man. You . . . !"

"Wrong!" gritted Dave. "He tried the sneak play. I've had a big plenty of this. Load him in that wagon and roll. Roll fast! If you don't . . . you'll never go. I tell you I'm fed up. Move . . . damn you . . . move!"

Dave's eyes were flaming, his face corded and white. The

Tremper boys knew deadly danger when they saw it. They did not argue any longer. They put a hurried bandage on Zeph Tremper's shoulder, loaded him in the wagon, and pulled out, heading for Boardman's Flat.

"I reckon you know best, Dave," said Jumbo. "But I think you made a mistake this time. We should have gunned the whole worthless crowd of them. They'll be back to make trouble, one way or another. Mark my word they'll be back."

"They've had their chance," said Dave bleakly. "If they stir up any more trouble for us, we'll finish it . . . for good."

CHAPTER TWELVE

They were across the creek from the Abbott wagon, on their way home. Dave was still grim and white from the experience with the Trempers. Yet despite the tumult of his feelings, he almost unconsciously glanced through an opening in the willows at the Abbott wagon. He saw Maidie, a queerly pathetic, humped little bundle, crouched on the wagon tongue, a rifle leaning beside her.

"Wait a minute," snapped Dave. "Something is wrong at the Abbott wagon."

"You know," said Tonto, "I thought I heard a shot from up here somewhere, just about the time we split up to close in on that Tremper outfit."

"Wait here," said Dave. "I'm going across."

Maidie lifted a tear-streaked, forlorn face as Dave came loping up. He stared at her.

"Maidie! What's the matter?"

"Oh, Dave," she gulped. "Your present . . . that beautiful little mare . . . over yonder . . . look!"

Dave dismounted, walked over to the dead animal. Maidie followed him, wan and dispirited. Dave turned to her. "There are a lot more horses in our cavvy herd," he said quietly. "There's a little pinto bronc' that will just suit you. But . . . how did it happen?"

"Estes . . . Lon Estes shot it."

"Estes! Why should he have killed that mare?"

Color crept into Maidie's wan face. "He was jealous . . . crazy jealous."

"Jealous! Who of?"

"Of you. Oh, I know it sounds terribly silly. But because you gave me that . . . that mare. And because I rode with you. He was like a wild man. And when I told him it was none of his business, he was like a mad thing. He saddled up, then shot the mare . . . then tore away, vowing he'd do the same thing to you. I . . . I went a little crazy myself. I got this rifle, and, if I could have gotten a shot at him, I'd have killed him. I wish I had," she ended fiercely.

Dave built a cigarette. "Tell me," he said gently, "what right has Estes to feel that way about you?"

"None at all, the murderous fool!" exclaimed Maidie. "I've never given him the slightest cause to imagine . . . imagine that I cared a snap of my fingers for him. You see, Dave . . . it was like this. On the drive in to Navajo River Meadows, Dad and I came across Lon Estes. His horse was dead and he was wounded, lying beside the trail. We didn't know who he was . . . had never seen him before. But just out of common decency, we picked him up, put him in the wagon, dressed his wound, and took care of him. He wasn't badly hurt. It was more thirst and loss of blood than anything. He got all right again, pretty quickly. But he wouldn't leave us. He'd been in Gallatin Basin before and he told Dad of this piece of ground along Cache Creek. He said it was as good a piece of land as there was in the basin. So Dad decided to try and get it. When we left Navajo River at the jump-off, Estes decided to come out ahead on horseback. He said he'd file on this ground and then turn it over to Dad, which he did and which we both thanked him for. That killing of one of the Trempers because he figured they were responsible for that knifing of Dad over beyond Vermilion Wall was his own idea entirely. Neither Dad nor I felt any too good about that killing. But we figured that Estes, in getting this piece of ground for us, was paying us back for helping him on the trail. That was all right. But . . . but when he started making love to me, well, I've been afraid of him secretly for some time. I . . . I told Dad I wished he would leave us . . . and Dad felt the same way. Yet, considering all he had done for us, we didn't want to tell him flat out. But today . . . when he began acting like he did, I got mad. I told him that the best thing he could do was to leave this camp and never come back. It was then he went berserk and killed my . . . my beautiful mare. Oh, Dave . . . I could weep and weep."

She put her hands over her face again. Dave patted her hunched shoulders. "Steady . . . steady," he said quietly. "I'll see that you get that little pinto bronc' I mentioned. And. . . ."

Maidie shook her head violently. "No! No . . . you mustn't ever give me another horse, Dave. You've got to stay away from me. That Estes, he's a deadly, venomous devil. He'd kill you, Dave. He would. And it would be my fault. And I think I'd die, if I was the cause of your . . . your. . . . No, Dave . . . you've been mighty good and kind to . . . to Dad and me. But you mustn't ever see or speak to me again."

Dave laughed curtly. "Bosh! Do you think for a minute I'd ever let any cheap tinhorn gunfighter tell me what I can or can't do? I don't scare that easy, Maidie. I'll take care of Estes when I meet him. Any man who would shoot down a horse in a fit of jealous madness isn't the sort to scare me. You're going to get that little pinto and you and me are going to be just as good friends as ever . . . maybe better. Don't you worry your pretty head no more."

Dave went back into his saddle and rode across the creek. In terse, cold words he told what had happened. "Why, the low-down, dirty coyote!" exploded Jumbo. "He ought to be mauled to an inch of his life."

"He's going to be," snapped Dave. "Tonto, you and me are going to Boardman's Flat. Buck, you and Jumbo go over, put your ropes on that dead bronc', and drag it out where the coyotes can clean it up. Tomorrow I bring that little Snake River pinto bronc' down for Maidie. Poor kid . . . she's broken-hearted."

Buck Custer shifted uneasily in his saddle. "You want to watch yourself, Dave with that Estes *hombre*. He's got all the earmarks. We don't know just how good or bad he is with a gun."

"I don't care, either," growled Dave. "I'm through talking and acting soft. We came into the basin figuring to try and get along peaceful and quiet with everybody. I can see now where this neck of the woods is a long, long way from the time when we can get along peaceful and quiet with anybody. From here on out, the Flying Diamond gets tough . . . tough as hell. If they won't let us alone when we treat 'em decent . . . then we put the fear of hell into 'em. Come on, Tonto."

The sun was westering rapidly when Dave and Tonto rode into Boardman's Flat. The dust that hung above the moiling street held a rose tint to it. But there was no like softness in the town. It was loud, blatant, uncouth. As they tied and left their horses, Tonto touched Dave on the arm.

"Better let me handle this Estes *hombre*, kid," he drawled. "I'm older at such a game than you, and maybe just a little more cautious. And while you're quite a bit more than a fair hand with a gun, I think I can say without braggin' that I'm still fast enough to shade you. And like Buck said, we don't know just how good this Estes is. The outfit . . . well, things would be pretty badly broken up, was he to get you."

Some of the bleakness left Dave's face for a moment. He spoke gruffly. "You old catamount. You ain't fooling me one little bit. I know what's in your mind. You'd get yourself shot for me. Well, it don't work out that way. And I don't figure to make this a shoot-out with Estes unless I have to. There is other medicine that hurts one of his stripe even more. He bullied and threatened a lone girl. And he shot a helpless bronc' through the head, just to show what a big, bad man he is. Wait until I get my hands on him."

They went along the streets steadily, but not hurried. Dave's face was bleak and rigid once more, his eyes stabbing alertly here and there. Tonto was equally watchful, his leathery old face unreadable, his eyes little bright, stabbing flecks.

They tried the saloons first, but saw nothing of Estes. A blare of music came from the newly constructed honky-tonk. Dave headed that way. The place was jammed, the bar crowded. Poker tables held a full complement of players. On a slightly raised floor at the rear the tinny piano was pounding, and several couples were dancing, the dance-hall girls garish with their flashy dresses.

Tonto jabbed an elbow into Dave's ribs. He pointed. "Yonder," he muttered.

Lon Estes was standing toward the lower end of the room, watching a stud game. Dave pushed a quiet way through the crowd and was within a stride of Estes before the gunman saw him. For one split second Estes looked startled. Then the hard film ran over his eyes; he drew a quick, hissing breath and snatched at his guns, trying to whirl aside as he did so.

Dave dove for him, his shoulder smashing into the gunman's chest, knocking him staggering. And then, before Estes could recover himself, Dave hit him with a sweeping right fist that knocked Estes flat.

Dave pounced, twisted the guns from Estes's dazed fists, sent them skittering across the floor. Then Dave stepped back, unbuckled his own gun belts, and passed them over his shoulder to Tonto.

"All right," he snapped. "Get on your feet, you dirty horse killer. You get a lesson now!"

Estes came up with startling speed, whining like some enraged animal. The speed suggested by his litheness was there, all right. He smashed Dave two wicked blows in the face before Dave could get his arms up. Dave staggered, while the heavy warmth of blood ran across his lips. But Dave side-stepped the gunman's next rush, shook his head, and was ready for Estes when he turned. He caught Estes coming in, with a straight-armed smash that knocked the gunman half across the poker table, which upset with a crash, in a welter of cursing men, flying cards, and scattered chairs.

Back came Estes again, his face running blood, his eyes blank with the killing rage of a crazed wolf. Dave met him and they stood toe to toe, slugging wickedly. They were about the same height, the same weight. But there was a certain raw-boned ruggedness to Dave, a rawhide toughness that Estes's speed and litheness could not master. The gunman threw the most punches, threw them faster, and the licking fury of them half blinded Dave. Yet when Dave's fists did find a mark on the gunman's body or face, there was a solid, crushing quality to them that more than made up for the superior speed of his opponent.

Remorselessly he drove Estes back, shaking him with short, solid hooks to the head and face, sickening and weakening him with pile-driver smashes to the body. After the first yell of alarm, when Estes had gone for his guns and the moment of cursing confusion caused by the upsetting of the poker table, the crowd had quieted, forming a solid circle about the two fighters, a circle that expanded and closed, writhed back and forth, following the movements of the fighters. Watching eyes were hot and savage with the lust of the thing. Men followed the punches with unconscious jerkings and jabs of their own fists, as though they were part of the fight themselves.

A bartender, fearing further damage to card tables and chairs, and fearing also that the thing might work into a general free-for-all that would completely wreck the joint, yelled something about stopping them. But a snarl of protest answered him.

"They're only a couple of those damned leather pants!" bellowed a settler. "Let 'em knock one another's brains out. Who gives a damn?"

Dance-hall girls, painted harpies that they were, pulled and mauled through the crowd to get a better view and began voicing shrill preferences between the two.

Dave Salkeld saw none of this, heard none of it. All he could see was this man in front of him, saw him through a crimson mist formed in part by his own streaming blood, and in part by the cold rage that convulsed him.

Two trip-hammer blows to the face shook Dave to his heels, but he answered with a blasting right fist under the heart that made Estes sag. Dave drove two more into the body, then switched with an overhand right that laid open a savage cut under the gunman's eye, knocking him completely back into the crowd, which held Estes on his feet and thrust him back. Estes, out on his feet, fell forward into a left hook that dropped him, shuddering and twitching, to the floor.

Dave stepped back, scrubbing his eyes clear of blood. He gulped hoarsely of the hot, thick air and waited for Estes to get up, his feet spread, his rock-hard fists swinging back and forth at his sides.

Estes tried to get up, he tried with a strained, terrible intentness. But there were limits beyond which the spirit could not drive the flesh. Estes was at that point now. He got as far as his knee, even got one booted foot under him. Then he fell over sideways.

Despite his flaming hatred for the gunman, Dave could not hold back a grudging admiration for the fellow. Whatever his other shortcomings, Lon Estes had courage.

A hulking teamster at the edge of the circle cursed sneeringly. He drove a heavy boot into the prone gunman's ribs. "Get up, you yellow whelp! Get up and show some guts!"

Dave took two strides and hit the teamster with every ounce of weight and remaining strength he had. The sound of his fist on the teamster's jaw was like the breaking of a board, and the teamster collapsed in a sprawled heap. The crowd yelled vociferous approval.

Lon Estes made another try to get up. This time he succeeded and stood swaying, his hands dangling helplessly at his sides. He seemed to be tensing himself in expectation of another blow. But Dave Salkeld stepped back, shaking his head.

"I'm no butcher," he panted thickly. "But I think you know where we stand, Estes. Don't ever get me after you again. The next time I'll kill you."

A thin, mirthless grimace of a smile twisted the gunman's battered face. That smile was more deadly than a scowl could possibly have been.

"Keno," he blurted hoarsely, "keno. We know where we stand. It had to be this way. I knew it the first time I laid eyes on you, Salkeld. Remember this one thing. From here on out, Gallatin Basin ain't big enough to hold you and me at the same time."

Saying which, Estes lurched past Dave and made his way through the loosening crowd to the bar. Here he called for whiskey and gulped it avidly.

Someone took Dave by the arm, steered him toward the door. It was Tonto. "We're getting out of town now," said Tonto. "That teamster you plastered might have some friends. And you've had about all the war you can stand for one day. Just why in hell did you hit that teamster anyway?"

"Because he kicked a man unable to defend himself," Dave growled. "Kicked a man with more nerve in his little finger than that damned muleskinner will ever have in his whole carcass. You can't take one thing away from Estes. He's got sand in his craw."

"Yeah." Tonto nodded. "And black poison in his heart. You've wrote yourself an obligation to kill, Dave. Either kill or be killed. That wolf will never rest now, until he's hung up your scalp to dry."

They stopped at the creek just out of town, where Dave washed the blood from his face and hands, bathed his bruises and cuts. Then they went into the saddle once more and left Boardman's Flat behind them at a fast lope.

CHAPTER THIRTEEN

Lon Estes put away nearly a pint of raw liquor before he quit drinking. Then he went behind the bar and took a bucket of water against the growled protest of a bartender, silencing that worthy's protests with a look that made the barkeep gulp and back away.

Estes washed up and was lithe and strong again as he recovered his guns from the floor where Dave Salkeld had thrown them. He looked them over carefully, shoved them into the holsters, and left the place. He got his horse and was riding out of town when he met up with another rider coming in. He threw a quick glance at the other horseman, stiffened, and pulled to a halt. His voice sounded thin and hard.

"Looking for somebody, Skagway?"

The other rider jerked to a halt, stared, then nodded, crossing his hands quickly on the horn of his saddle. "Yeah," he croaked. "Looking for you, Lon. Wolf Rossiter heard you were somewhere in this basin, so he sent me out to. . . ."

"Wolf Rossiter! What's he doing in Gallatin Basin?"

Skagway, a gangling, slouchy sort, with a loose mouth above a receding chin, shrugged and turned his hands up, a leering smirk on his face. "What does Wolf Rossiter land in any territory for? Not just for the ride, you can bet on that."

"And what does he want of me?"

"I don't know for shore. Maybe to make you some kind of a proposition. Anyway, he said that, if I located you, I was to tell you that he was willing to let bygones be bygones. He's not holding any grudge and he wants to talk business with you. What the hell happened to your face? You look like you'd had a heart-to-heart talk with a grizzly bear."

"Never mind my face," snarled Estes. "Where is Rossiter?"

Skagway jerked a head toward the Windy Mountains. "Him and the rest of the boys are holed up in a cañon back there."

Estes stared a long time at the mountains. Then he twisted in his saddle and looked off to the northeast in the direction of Cache Creek. For a brief moment a shadow of indecision crossed his battered face. Then that look was gone, replaced by the old, thin, harsh bleakness, while his eyes, behind their puffed and darkening lids, turned feral and cold.

"All right," he snapped. "I'll ride with you. Come on."

"Wait a minute . . . wait a minute," protested Skagway. "I got to get some liquor for the boys. If I went back without it, and some smoking, they'd skin me alive."

Estes jerked his head. "Go on in and get it. But don't go making a bender of it for yourself. I'll give you fifteen minutes, no longer."

"That'll be long enough," promised Skagway uneasily, using his spurs. "I'll be back."

He was, a loaded gunny sack tied across his saddle cantle. They struck out, straight for the Windies. The sun was down now, buried in a sea of blazing scarlet and gold. The blue tide of evening filled Gallatin Basin and washed up the lower slopes of the Windies. Only on the highest peaks did the sunset light still hold and this was more reflection than anything else.

It was dark by the time they plunged into the timber, but Skagway seemed to know where he was going. They crossed the timbered face of a ponderous slope and plunged into the inky blackness of a cañon mouth. Skagway clung to the left slope of the cañon as it wound deeper and deeper back into the heart of the mountains. Below and on their right they could hear the muffled tumult of a foaming stream and the air that drifted up to them was chill and damp.

In time the steep slope of the cañon walls lessened, widening out into a long meadow, marked here and there with black clumps of timber, the tips of which were silvered by the light of the stars. By one of these timber clumps a fire burned, the smoke of it a winnowing, pungent veil in the still, heavy air.

As Estes and Skagway rode up, furtive figures slipped away from the firelight and a harsh hail came out of the darkness at them.

"That you, Skag?"

"Yeah," answered Skagway. "Everything is OK, Wolf. I got Estes with me. He's willing to talk business."

They dismounted and walked up to the fire. Wariness lay in every move of Estes. His voice rang, thin and hard. "If you're on the square, Rossiter . . . you'll move into the firelight first."

There sounded a laugh and a hulking, raw-boned figure stepped close to the flames. "Still the same old Estes, eh?" said Rossiter. "Well, that's all right. And I'm on the square. Here's my hand on it. We should never have rowed in the first place, you and me. We can be too valuable to each other."

Estes prowled up to him and there was a brief handshake. Other men moved in from the darkness to the firelight.

"The same old crowd, with a couple of real additions. You know the older boys, Lon. Shake hands with Nick Lamont and Pete Washoe. They'll do to ride with. Purdy, rustle some grub for Lon and Skag. Sa-ay . . . what happened to your face, Lon?"

"My business," snapped Estes. "Skagway said you had a proposition. What is it?"

"You and Skag eat first, then we'll break out a bottle and talk it over."

Wolf Rossiter was a big man, his high shoulders suggesting a

126

tremendous, clumsy power. His face was big and bony, high, prominent cheek bones seeming to pinch his pale eyes against either side of a big, jutting nose. A puckered scar pulled one corner of his mouth down and seemed to put his pointed chin out of balance with the rest of his features. His expression, even in relaxation, was strangely vulpine and sinister.

When Estes finished eating, he leaned back on one elbow and built a cigarette. "Shoot," he said tersely.

Rossiter jerked his head. "Any money in the basin?"

Estes laughed. "Money! Lousy with it. Two-thirds of the settlers and sodbusters left another layout somewhere before coming into Gallatin Basin to stake a new homestead. All of those got a fat sock stowed away in their wagons. Of course, there are some who haven't got a thing beyond their wagon, broncos, and the clothes on their back, regular, drifting sodbusters who never light long in any one place. Expecting to find a gold mine waiting for them to pick up and starving to death while they look for it. But there is plenty of money in that basin. Why?"

Wolf Rossiter's laugh was just a gulping inhalation of breath. "You ought to know why, Lon. If there's money in the basin, me and the boys are interested in it. They got the law and order bug yet?"

"Hell, no. They're a full year away from that stage at least."

"We ought to be able to do a right smart bit of hustling in a year," murmured Rossiter. "Want to sit in with us, Lon?"

Estes inhaled deeply. "I might. How do you figure to work?"

"Night work. Pick a wagon and hit it while they sleep. Then slice off in another direction and hit another pickup. We can land a dozen or so in a single night. Then, while they're all stampeded and loco in one part of the basin, we'll hit another part the next night and work the same. Gallatin is a big basin, and I reckon there are lots of wagons."

"Hundreds of 'em," agreed Estes. "How'll we share?"

"Share and share alike, all through our crowd."

Estes did not hesitate. "Write me in on it. I'll ride with you."

"Good!" exclaimed Rossiter. "We'll drink on that." Then: "Any cattle in the basin?"

"Two outfits. The C Cross, owned by a Luke Converse, and the Flying Diamond, with two partners, Salkeld and Custer. We don't need to worry about them now. They're going to be fighting one another before long. And later, Wolf, when we've cleaned out the settlers, we'll have a look at those two herds. By that time the two outfits should be weakened pretty bad, fighting each other. We roll over them, bunch the herds, and drive out to some place like Aspen City. We ought to be able to turn the cattle over for a pretty penny. Sound all right to you?"

"It sounds great to me," enthused Rossiter. "We'll have another drink on that, Lon. I told you we were too valuable to each other not to be riding the same trail."

The stars hung, high and thin and pale, over Gallatin Basin. On a little creek toward the northern end of the basin, as yet unnamed, a settler's wagon stood, dark and quiet. A team of horses, picketed a little distance apart from the wagon, dozed shot-hipped under the stars. Under the wagon, a blanketed figure, slept the settler, weary from a day of honest toil on virgin land that held his future. In the wagon slept his wife and two small children.

Both on the east and the west the slopes ran down rather sharply to the creek. A coyote, slinking along the ridge top to the east, about to put its muzzle to the stars and wail its age-old song, crouched in sudden alarm as the muffled tempo of many hoofs came rolling out of the east. The coyote flattened and fled like a shadow into the night. Up to the ridge top moved a dark mass of mounted men.

One of the settler's horses stirred nervously, snorted and

stamped. The sleeping settler awoke, raised on one elbow, looked and listened. One moment the night was still. Then, like a rush of sudden thunder, hard-spurring riders came catapulting down the slope.

The settler fought clear of his blankets, rolled from under the wagon, surged erect, grabbed the rifle leaning against a rear wheel. He got off one hurried shot, too hurried, for it flew high and wild. The pencil of flame from his weapon marked him. A roll of gunfire answered him, and he sank quietly and limply back to the dew-moistened earth, torn through and through with murderous lead.

A thin cry of fright came from the woman in the wagon, the wail of an awakened child. Men clambered over the tailgate of the wagon, seized the woman and her children, threatened them with savage brutality, almost threw them from the wagon. One of the raiders cursed at the woman.

"Keep your yap shut or you get the same as your man!"

The youngest child wailed again in fright and the man struck swiftly at it. But the mother, dazed and stupefied, acted instinctively. She threw out a protecting arm and took the blow herself. The brute cursed and would have struck again, but a snarling order from someone else sent him clambering back into the wagon.

Food, blankets, all kinds of frugal equipment was tossed helter-skelter from the wagon. Match light threw little splotches of dimly sinister glow through the canvas top. Curses of thwarted greed came from the wagon.

"Not a damned thing in here," growled a renegade. "Make that woman tell us where it is."

Another renegade who had been going over the crumpled figure of the settler with rough hands exclaimed in triumph: "Here it is, boys! The damned sodbuster had a money belt. Come on . . . I got it. Let's ride."

Horses whirled and snorted and men went back into their saddles. The ground shook under the pound of hoofs. Then they were gone, farther north. Soon there was no further sound of them. The night was still, while the horrified stars seemed to draw farther and farther back into the shelter of the heavens. The woman was like a crouched statue, her children drawn into the shelter of her arms, her face a still, haggard mask of grief and lonely hopelessness. . . .

Half an hour later, faintly from the north, came another short burst of firing. Later still the sound of guns echoed to the northwest. Then twice, at wide intervals, from the west. And just at dawn a gangling youth of twelve, up on a bony work horse that was never meant for speed, galloped heavily toward Boardman's Flat, crying the alarm to each startled settler camp he passed.

Up on the north fork of Cache Creek, the Flying Diamond crew was preparing to guard against any further slow-elking trouble. The whole outfit spent two days up in the summer range basin above Painted Rock, building a small but stout cabin in the timber island by the spring. Food and blankets were carried in and two men detailed to stay there and keep an eye on things. These two were brothers, Ed and Jerry Pike, lean, brown, grave-faced men, staunch and dependable.

Dave Salkeld gave them their parting instructions. "Your work will amount only to watching and riding, boys. Carry saddle guns all the time and ride together. If you run into any trouble, don't waste words or lead. We'll back any stand you take. And just so we'll know that everything is all right, ride down to headquarters a couple of times a week and report."

The next morning Dave was up early. Still in his mind was his promise to take another pony down to Maidie Abbott, that pinto, the Snake River bronco. The horse had not been ridden much lately, so he decided to put a saddle on it and see how the animal handled.

The pinto did a mite of pitching at first, but soon cooled off. Dave rode it up and down the creek a few times, judging its gait. The pinto was a sound little beast, with a good, intelligent head. Dave nodded in satisfaction. An honest horse, the pinto, and smart. Spirited, but easy to handle. Under Maidie's affection and treatment, it would soon become a docile pet.

Up at headquarters sounded the mellow *jangle* of Mose's breakfast gong and Dave was just about to turn and ride back when his eye caught a flicker of movement just beyond a point of willow some 200 yards below. As he watched, a stripling figure in overalls stumbled into view, staggering with exhaustion. The first glint of the rising sun cast a golden hue on the bared head of that figure, and recognition struck Dave like a physical blow.

"Maidie!" he exclaimed. "Maidie Abbott!"

He lifted the startled pinto into a scudding run and tore down to the girl. As she glimpsed Dave's approach, the girl sank down in a little heap. Dave left his saddle with a leap, caught the girl by the arms, and lifted her to her feet.

"Maidie . . . what's wrong?" He shook her slightly.

She was almost too exhausted to answer. Her face was stained with tears. Her head rolled slightly.

"Dave," she gasped weakly. "Dave. They're coming after you . . . after you and your crew. They mean to kill you, Dave. . . ."

"Wait a minute," said Dave sternly. "Let me get this straight. Who's coming to kill me and my crew?"

"The . . . the settlers. They've been gathering down below, ever since dark last night. Dad . . . he's been trying to talk sense to them, but they are wild and savage and they won't listen.

131

I . . . I watched my chance and came to warn you. Oh, Dave . . . I thought I never would get here."

CHAPTER FOURTEEN

Dave lifted the distraught girl into the saddle, got up behind her, and sped for headquarters. Buck Custer and the other boys were just entering the cook shack when Dave thundered up. They stared in amazement at the white-faced girl. "What the devil . . . ?" began Buck Custer.

"Lift her down, Buck," cut in Dave. "She's brought us a warning of some kind. Take her inside and get some hot coffee into her. Looks like she came all the way from the main creek on foot. She's all in, poor kid."

The stimulation of hot coffee and a short rest brought Maidie to coherency. And she told the grim-faced circle of listeners a wicked and terrible story.

She told of night riders who had swept over a section of the Gallatin Basin, surprising lone settlers in their sleep, shooting, killing, robbing. "I don't know why," she ended, "but you men are suspected. I heard them talking. They started gathering down by our wagon last night. There must be a hundred of them by this time. They had ropes, guns. They must have suspected that I would warn you, for several times, when I started to leave camp, one of them stopped me and sent me back. But I got away finally and . . . and . . . they can't be far behind."

Dave patted her shoulder wordlessly as he looked at the crew. "We can't let them get as far as this headquarters, or they'll wreck everything we've slaved to build. Why those wild fools should think we did any raiding, I don't know. But we've got to stop them first and argue later. We'll stop 'em in the gap. Catch and saddle . . . and take saddle guns. Hike, boys . . . we can't let 'em get past the gap."

The crew rushed out, forgetting all about their morning meal. Dave took both of Maidie's limp hands in his own. "Someday we'll make all this up to you and your father," he said gently. "As for you, I salute as game and stout a little lady as ever breathed. You stay here with Mose until we get back. Mose, guard this girl with your life."

Mose, his wide smile missing for once, nodded steadily. "Marse Dave, anybody tries to lay one finger on that li'l missy, he sho' gotta climb over ole Mose's daid body to git dere. That's sho' nuff gospel. Missy, you stay right along here with ole Mose. He git yo' hot water to wash yo' pore li'l face. He give yo' hot breakfast, and he keep yo' safe as safe can be."

Dave and his men spurred downcreek at a hurtling run. But even as they entered the narrow gap that led from their own smaller basin to the great basin beyond, they got their first glimpse of the approaching settler horde.

The settlers had just entered the lower end of the gap. Some had horses—most were afoot. All of them were armed with some sort of weapon. As they sighted the Flying Diamond crew, a deep, sullenly threatening shout rolled from them. They came on steadily, brandishing their weapons, yelling threats.

Dave snapped terse orders. "Spread across the gap, boys. Don't give an inch. Whatever you do, don't shoot unless I tell you to. We can't let this thing come to a battle, for our own sake as well as theirs. We've got to make them stop and parley. Buck, you and I go out to meet them. Come on."

The cowboys scattered across the gap, a thin line of defenders, but a grim and stalwart one, silent, watchful, but indomitable. Despite their overwhelming superiority of numbers, the advancing settlers slowed. It was one thing to make talk of wiping out the Flying Diamond crew. But it was entirely something else again actually to accomplish that end. The settlers were beginning to realize this as they looked over those silent, watchful cowboys.

Dave rode with his right hand thrown high, palm ahead, in the age-old peace sign of the wilderness. And he called out, his voice cutting coldly and sharply through the rumble of the mob: "We don't know what this is all about! But one thing is shore. You don't go through this gap while a single man of the Flying Diamond is able to fire a last shot. It'll be bloody if you try it. Better stop and think it over . . . and talk. Who's leading you?"

The settler horde, clumsy and ponderous, slowed to an uneasy halt. From the rear ranks, savage shouts and taunts were thrown. Dave ignored them. "Who's leading you?" he yelled again.

A gaunt settler with a black beard and deep-set, grief-chilled eyes moved out. "I am," he growled. "And talking won't do any good. We're coming through, and be damned to you."

"That is an argument I hope we don't have to settle with guns," retorted Dave. "Suppose, just for appearance sake, you state your case. What is the reason for all this?"

"You know the reason," snarled the bearded man. "Riding in the night like a bunch of bloody wolves, murdering, robbing, shooting up lone wagons. Do you think we settlers are going to stand for that? You damned cattlemen . . . you'd like nothing better than to get Gallatin Basin all to yourselves, to run your damned cows on. You think a settler, a man with a family, hasn't a right in the world to free land. From the time the first settler drove the first wagon into the open range, you cattlemen have persecuted him. You've murdered and threatened and used every scheme you could to keep him from finding a piece of land to earn a living on. You've wanted to hog all the range from the beginning. Well, it don't go here. The settlers in Gallatin Basin will fight you to the last damned inch. And for every raid a cattleman throws at us, we throw two back at him. This is one showdown where the settler comes into his own."

A deep-throated shout rolled through the ranks of the settlers. They started to move ahead again. But Dave held his ground. And now, out beside the bearded settler moved another man. It was Jim Abbott. He grabbed the bearded man by the arm. "Slow those damned fools down!" he yelled. "I tell you for the last time, Stinson . . . you're barking up the wrong tree in suspecting Dave Salkeld and his men. They're white men, decent men. They're not the kind of damned wolves who pulled that raid. Watch yourself that you don't lead these fools into something you'll put in the rest of your life being sorry for."

Stinson hesitated, then turned and faced the settler horde, both arms thrown high. "Slow down!" he shouted. "We'll hear what Salkeld has to say!"

The ominous advance halted again. Dave swung from his saddle, squatted on his heels, and built a cigarette. "It is easier to talk and understand one another this way," he said. "Suppose you go into a little detail, Stinson."

"They're bloody, and reeking of hell," said Stinson somberly, staring at Dave with his deep eyes. "They murdered Abner Jones, robbed him . . . left his wife a widow, his two children without a father. They killed Claus Drinkwater, wounded his wife slightly, and gun-whipped his ten-year-old boy senseless. Then they robbed. They killed and robbed Tom Curtis. They robbed Henry Steves and left him for dead. Maybe he will die. I saw him and he's bad off. Then they struck my brother's wagon. He had heard the shooting at the Steves' wagon and he was awake when they rushed him. He fought them off for a minute. Then they riddled his wagon with lead. They killed my brother, they killed his wife, they killed his baby boy."

Stinson's lips were twitching as he ended, his eyes were burning with a sick grief.

Dave came to his feet. "Look at me, Stinson," he said gravely. "I know exactly how you must feel. You've got my sincere sympathy. But clear your eyes and look at me . . . hard. Now tell me . . . do you think I'm the kind of man who would do the things you have just told me of? Do I look like a cowardly murderer of helpless men and women and babies in arms? Good God, man! Do you realize what you are charging me and my riders with?"

Listening to Dave's ringing words, the settler horde went very still. Stinson stared at Dave, licked his twitching lips slowly. His shaggy head dropped. "Sorry," he mumbled thickly. "Sorry, Salkeld. You're right. You couldn't have done such a thing. But . . . but I guess I've been . . . half loco. . . ."

Dave dropped a hand on Stinson's shoulder. "Thanks," he said simply. "What you've seen would drive any man loco."

A venomous voice sounded from the ranks of the settlers. "Don't let him soft-soap you, Stinson. I'm telling you this damned Flying Diamond is responsible for those killings and robberies. Din't they try and drive me and my boys out of Gallatin? Damned right they did. Ask him about that and see what kind of a lie he tells."

Jim Abbott let out a savage growl, dived into the crowd, and emerged, dragging the spitting, squirming, snarling figure of Zeph Tremper by the scruff of the neck.

"You poisonous old hellcat," growled Abbott. "I've had a big plenty of you. You were the one who first started talk that Salkeld and his men were responsible for those raids. Now, damn you . . . you're face to face with the man you accuse. We'll see where you stand."

Zeph Tremper tried to twist free, but Jim Abbott shook him

until his teeth chattered. After that he stood, sullen and scowling. Dave Salkeld looked at him coldly.

"Yeah," he said, "we did tell Tremper to take his litter and get out of Gallatin Basin. 'Cause why? Because we caught the three Tremper boys red-handed, slow-elking one of the Flying Diamond beeves. Because they've been troublemakers from the first. Clear back at Navajo River Meadows, before the jump-off, they made trouble. That is all they know how to do . . . raise hell of some sort."

"I can back that up," said Jim Abbott. "I've had my trouble with 'em. They did their damnedest to knife me while I slept, because I wouldn't let 'em bluff me out of the use of the forge back at Navajo River. They ought to be run out of the basin."

Dave spoke again, raising his voice so that it might reach many ears. "I know all about the age-old quarrel between the settler and the cattleman. I want none of it. I never have wanted any of it. Fighting of any kind wastes a man's substance. When my partner and I first thought of coming to Gallatin Basin with our herd, we talked the whole thing over mighty careful. We knew there would be hundreds of you men come to Gallatin. We knew we had no right to try and get and hold bottom land range. So we made a trip in here a month before the rush. We looked the whole basin over. We decided that we could move in on the north fork of Cache Creek, up in the foothills, where the grazing is good, but the land no use for farming or growing things. We made up our minds that we'd have no quarrel with you settlers. All we wanted and still want is to go ahead quietly, minding our own business, harming no man. I want you to believe this one thing, and go on believing it. We want to be friends with every decent man in Gallatin Basin."

A murmur went through the settlers. Heads nodded slowly. "That's straight talk," said one of them. "I remember when they brought their herd across the basin. Salkeld and one of his men rode ahead, giving out word that the cattle were crossing, promising there would be no attempt at stopping the cattle down in the bottom lands. They kept that word. Now that I've cooled off, I think we're chasing the wrong 'coon. My vote is to go on back and talk things over and be a little more shore of ourselves before we start on the warpath again."

The idea took hold, ran through the crowd. Stinson held out his hand. "Sorry, Salkeld. I'm shore we were wrong now."

Zeph Tremper snarled and Stinson whirled on him. "Enough out of you, Tremper," he growled. "Salkeld is right . . . so is Jim Abbott. You and your boys are no damned good. Now I'm telling you to gather 'em up and get out of Gallatin. Your damned poisonous talk started us off on something that might have been hell for all of us. You did it to serve your own hate. You're rotten, Tremper. Get out of my sight!"

Tremper slinked back through the crowd, met by growls and curses along the way. When he got clear of the crowd, he hurried off downstream like a sidling, venomous old wolf.

The settlers started to break up, but halted when Dave Salkeld raised his arm and spoke again. "Me and my men hate night riders as bad as you do. To show you how we feel about this, I make this offer. We'll be ready to ride at all times. Scrape up a messenger on a fast horse, and, if you can get word to us when the next raid strikes . . . and I think there'll be more of them . . . we'll ride and see what we can do about it. We've got good horses and we'll cover ground as fast as the raiders can. And if we can run them into a fight, we'll more than even up for what they've done. We're with you all the way in stamping out these night riders. Is that fair?"

"It's more than fair!" yelled a man. "You're all right, Salkeld. I'm more than apologizing for my part in this. Now I'm going home."

There was no more truculence or indecision. The settlers

began straggling back down the creek. Dave turned to Stinson. "The women and kids of those murdered men . . . they can eat Flying Diamond beef as long as they need it. Send a man up here later today with a couple of pack horses. I'll have the boys cut a beef out and slaughter it and the meat will go down to those folks who need it."

"You make me feel like a dawg, Salkeld," said Stinson simply. "For the sake of those women and kids . . . I accept. I'll send a man for that meat."

He tramped away, a gaunt man with bowed shoulders.

"You come back to the ranch with us, Jim," Dave told Abbott. "Maidie is there. She warned us. You can be proud of that girl."

Dave Salkeld gave no explanation to his riders until they were back at headquarters and gathered in the bunkhouse. Then he told them of the night riders and what they had done. "I'm human," he ended up harshly. "I don't care whether those poor unfortunate folks are sodbusters or not. Women were widowed, kids were half orphaned, left without a father or any money. One kid was gun-whipped, cruel. At least one woman and one baby were killed. I'm not made to stand that sort of thing. I pledged the aid of the Flying Diamond outfit to knock hell out of those damned night riders. How do you boys feel about it?"

"There's only one way to feel," rumbled Jumbo. "Like men. I ask nothing better than to get a chance at those murdering rats. We'll follow you through hell, Dave . . . to get a crack at 'em."

There wasn't a single word of dissent to this.

"All right, boys . . . that is set," said Dave. "Keep the fastest bronc' in your string fresh and ready at all times. Keep your guns oiled and plenty of shells in your belts and saddlebags. We'll show the settlers in Gallatin Basin that there is one cattle outfit they can trust and swear by."

"Do you think it could have been Converse and his crowd?" asked Wampus.

Dave shrugged. "Who knows? Though I don't think so. Converse is more interested in getting some range for his cattle. From all I can hear, he's got his herd back south along the Windies somewhere. But the feed isn't much down there. We'll have our troubles with Converse when he gets desperate enough to try and break in on this end."

Dave and Tonto and Jumbo rode back with Jim and Maidie Abbott to the Abbott wagon. Maidie was up on the pinto bronco. She was still wan and pale. But the fulsomeness of praise she had gotten from all of the Flying Diamond boys had put a glow in her eyes.

"You're mighty good neighbors, Jim . . . you and Maidie," said Dave as they halted at the camp. "Anything the Flying Diamond can ever do for you, won't have to be asked for twice. But I'm going to be worried about you two until we smash these night riders. I'd feel easier if you'd spend your nights up at the ranch. It isn't so far, when you've got horses. You'd be more than welcome."

Abbott looked at him steadily. "Thanks, Dave. Maybe we'll take you up on that. I admit I'm worried, not for myself . . . but for Maidie. Especially after that incident with Estes."

Dave's eyes narrowed. "You think Estes is mixed up with these night riders?"

Abbott shrugged. "Estes is a strange man, full of dark, secret currents. There is good in him, strange as that may sound to you, and a capacity for black hell, once he is aroused. He is one of those kind of unfortunate men with tempers that burn them to a cinder. When the black devils are riding him, I wouldn't put anything beyond him. Since he's pulled out, I've been relieved, yet afraid."

"I know what you mean. Simplest answer to that is that you

do as I suggest. Spend your nights at the ranch . . . at least until you get your cabin built. When do you expect to get started?"

"I go for lumber tomorrow. Maidie and I will see you at the ranch tonight."

Maidie waved to them as they rode away, heading for Boardman's Flat.

CHAPTER FIFTEEN

Boardman's Flat was in the grip of wild excitement. News of the night raids had scattered to the far reaches of Gallatin Basin. The town was full of settlers, truculent, worried, savage. Jim Boardman had sold out about every box of rifle and pistol ammunition in the place. Even in the street, settlers carried rifles over their arms. The air was tense, explosive. And Jim Boardman was fit to be tied. An hour previous a man half dead from wounds, clinging to an exhausted horse, had dashed into town, staggered in to see Boardman. He brought news of a raid on one of Boardman's pack trains, coming in from Aspen City. The raid had taken place far back in the Windies, where the pack train had been trapped in a narrow cañon and shot to pieces. One survivor, the man who brought news of the affair, escaped.

He had nothing to tell beyond the actual occurrence of the raid. It had been so sudden and devastating and deadly. The raiders had been hidden along the cañon rim, the pack train men caught like rats in a trap.

When Dave and Tonto and Jumbo heard the news, they went to see Boardman, found him craggy and harsh. "If I only had some idea of who those skunks could have been," he kept saying over and over again.

"Maybe the same gang that raided those settler wagons, Jim," suggested Dave. "They may be holed out back in the mountains somewhere and in need of grub. And raiding one of your pack trains was the easiest way they could figure out to get it. Just

where does the pack train come through?"

Boardman led the way into the street, then pointed at the misty mountains. "See that split peak dead east of here? Well, the trail comes around the south shoulder of that split peak. From what I could get from pore Jeff Soames, the raid took place just this side the peak, where the trail drops down through a cañon. It is rough country in there, laced full of cañons of one sort or another. The dirty rats! This basin is going to catch plenty of hell before it gets civilized, Salkeld."

"Couldn't have been Converse, do you think, Boardman?" asked Tonto.

Boardman shook his head. "No. Converse sent a man in yesterday for two pack horse loads of grub. He's having trouble enough finding range for his cattle down at the south end of the basin, without trying any other kind of action. No . . . it wasn't Converse."

"Then it leaves only one answer," said Tonto. "Some other gang we know nothing about has holed up in the mountains and is set to prey on the basin. This means wild times ahead."

"Ahead," snorted Boardman. "They're here now, cowboy. Here . . . plenty!"

It did not take long for the news of the raid on Boardman's pack train to reach the street, and it added just one more chunk of fuel to the fire of excitement and worry that burned among the settlers and other men who crowded the town. Plenty of scowls and black looks followed Dave and his two companions as they sauntered about.

"These cussed sodbusters still look at us like we were a flock of bloody-handed mavericks," mumbled Jumbo. "Dog-goned if it ain't beginning to get on my nerves, Dave. Maybe we ought to stay home and keep away from this town when things are stewin' the way they are."

"No, not that, Jumbo," said Dave. "I had two ideas in coming

144

to town. One was to see if we could hear anything that might give us a lead on who's responsible for those raids. The other is to show ourselves among the settlers so they'll get used to us and quit being on the peck every time we show our faces. Were we to hole up at the ranch and never show ourselves, it would only make them more suspicious. Say . . . there's Stinson, the leader of that gang who came after us this morning. Hi, Stinson!"

The bearded settler who was hurrying about on some sort of business came over to them. "Hello, boys," he said gravely. "I've sent a man after that beef you promised."

"Good." Dave nodded. "He'll find the meat all hung up and cooled out. Anything new, besides that raid on Boardman's pack train?"

"Some of us are getting a gang rounded up for a mass meeting in the Free Land Saloon," explained Stinson. "We aim to raise a little money to divide among the women and kids of those wagons that were raided. Bill Broom offered us the use of his saloon. Meeting will be called in about fifteen minutes, if you care to listen in."

Stinson hurried away, speaking to this man and that as he went along.

"I wish 'em luck and a big collection," said Jumbo. "But me, I got no hankering to get caught in that saloon with a flock of sodbusters around. They might get ideas toward a poor lone cowboy."

"Wrong again, Jumbo." Dave grinned. "We're going to be right up front at that meeting. Come on."

By the time they reached the Free Land Saloon, they found the place so jammed, they had to be content with a place near the door. The bar was doing a rushing business and the rumble of talk filled the place with a steady hum.

A few yards up along the bar stood two men in riding equipment. There was a hard-faced, narrow-eyed watchfulness about them. Tonto jabbed an elbow at Dave, nodded his head. "Ever see those two *hombres* before, Dave?" he murmured.

Dave shook his head. "Saddle men, all right . . . but I don't recall them. May be some of Converse's crew. Here comes Stinson."

The bearded settler went behind the bar and spoke to a fat, red-faced man, who nodded and proceeded to pound on the bar with a bung starter. "Quiet down, you coyotes!" he yelled. "Dan Stinson has something to tell you! Shut up and listen!"

The room quieted as Stinson climbed up and stood on the bar. "I'm not going into any detail," said Stinson. "All you fellows know what happened last night as well as I do. Bill Broom here was good enough to let us use his place, so we don't want to clutter it up any longer than we have to. That raid last night left some women and kids without any provider, without any money. We aim to collect a little money to help tide those women and kids along. Some of the boys are going to circulate around with open hats. I want to see you drop as much money in those hats as you can afford to give. That's all."

"Don't be afraid to open up!" yelled red-faced Bill Broom. "It is our responsibility to take care of those women and kids. I'm starting the ball rolling with a hundred dollars . . . in gold. Here it is, Dan."

The heavy coins *clinked* into Stinson's hat. The bartender at Bill Broom's right dropped in another golden double eagle. At Stinson's nod, half a dozen other men began working through the crowd. Coins *clinked* into open hats. A stony-faced gambler at one of the poker tables, with several stacks of gold coins in front of him, swept a solid stack in a proffered hat.

"Let's hear that money clink, boys!" bellowed Bill Broom. "Open up your hearts and your pockets. Show those poor unfortunate folks that Gallatin Basin knows how. Every man who contributes gets a free drink on the house."

"One thing I could never figure," mumbled Jumbo. "A saloon owner will feed likker to some poor, benighted drunk until he's got every cent the drunk owns. Then he'll turn right around and give it away to somebody else. Human nature shore has me licked at times."

"I reckon," drawled Tonto, "that he figgers one angle as a matter of business, while the other is just being a human being."

Dan Stinson, working through the crowd by the door, started to pass Dave and Tonto and Jumbo. "Wait a minute, Dan," said Dave. "Ain't our money any good?"

"You boys have already given more than your share, in that free beef," said Stinson.

"Nothing doing. That beef was from the outfit. This is from us." Dave dropped a handful of coins into Stinson's hat, and Tonto and Jumbo followed suit. "That money will buy food for those women and kids," said Jumbo. "Where, most likely, it would only buy me a headache and a bad taste in my mouth. Take it and welcome, Stinson."

Stinson moved on, coming presently to the two strange, hard-faced riders at the bar. They eyed the proffered hat a trifle sullenly, then shrugged and reached for their pockets. One of them brought out a miscellany of coins, pocket knife, and other odds and ends. Stinson watched him sorting the coins, and suddenly he stiffened and grew very still. For among the coins there was a ring, a heavy gold ring, fashioned in the form of two serpents, twined one about the other, the flattened heads reared upright to form the seal. It was plainly hand-wrought and was badly worn.

Stinson's words erupted from him in savage harshness. "That ring . . . where did you get it? Quick! Where did you get my brother's ring?"

The rider cursed thinly and his answer was as savage as it was unexpected. He jerked a gun and smashed Stinson over the head with it. Stinson went down, but not out.

"Stop them . . . stop those two!" he yelled thickly. "Don't let 'em get away. They're raiders! One has my dead brother's ring! Stop them!"

The two hard-faced riders were driving toward the door, blistering curses. One drove two thunderous shots into the floor and the dazed and startled crowd of settlers gave back in wild confusion, too slow-witted to get the import of Dan Stinson's shouted words.

But Dave Salkeld understood. As did Tonto Rice and Jumbo Curtis. As an open avenue showed to the door and the two renegades started along it, they found that avenue suddenly blocked by three crouched figures in chaps and broad hats.

The frantic renegades did not hesitate. Their guns began to leap and *thud,* and were answered by tongues of pale flame and gusts of smoke blooming at the hips of Dave and his two staunch and faithful companions.

The leading renegade, the one who had had the ring, seemed to stumble over nothing and went down in a sliding fall, choking queerly. The second came on, however, like a desperate, trapped animal, rolling both guns as he ran. Tonto cursed as a slug smashed his left hand, hurling the gun from it. The shock seemed to paralyze Tonto for a moment, so that his other gun hand hung stiff and useless.

But Dave and Jumbo were still shooting, intent and deadly. And, of a sudden, the second renegade seemed to strike an invisible wall of stone, for he halted in full stride, rocked a moment, then went stumbling backward, finally to fall flat on his shoulders, his eyes dead and unseeing as he struck the floor.

The saloon was in a wild uproar. Many of those at the back of the room had no idea what the shooting was all about. When they finally did break into the clear, they saw Dave and Jumbo just holstering their smoking guns. They drew a mistaken inference.

"Those damned leather pants again!" yelled someone. "They've shot up a couple more pore devils . . . !"

Then Dan Stinson was on his feet and roaring. "Calm down, you fools! These cowboys stopped two of the dirty murderers who were in that raid. Calm down!"

A smear of blood was seeping down the side of Dan Stinson's head. He looked about on the floor, picked up something, and nodded as he held it out on his hand. "Boys," he said, his voice deep and moving, "I'll never be able to even up with you. You got at least two of the murderers of my brother and his family. I gave this ring to my brother Jim myself. He didn't wear it much, but kept it in his poke all the time."

The crowd, getting the truth at last, came surging around to offer congratulations. But Dave turned to Jumbo. "Take Tonto to a doctor, Jumbo," he said grimly. "Tonto, how bad is that hand?"

"Not too bad," was the cool answer. "That was nice gun work, kid . . . that you and Jumbo put on."

Jumbo led Tonto away and Dave Salkeld dropped on one knee to look over the two dead renegades. He looked up at the milling, staring crowd. "Anybody ever see these two *hombres* before?" he demanded.

No one had, apparently, so Dave went out in search of Tonto and Jumbo. He found them presently, coming out of one of the new, raw-boarded cabins. Tonto's hand was swathed in new white bandages. Catching Dave's glance, Tonto spoke easily.

"The doc said it was close, Dave . . . but that the flipper should be as good as new in a couple of weeks. Get any line on who those two coyotes were?"

"No, but it's a cinch they must have been part of that raiding gang. Dan Stinson positively identified that ring one of 'em had. I figure the two were sent down here by their chief to see what the reaction of the basin was to that raid."

"Shouldn't wonder," agreed Tonto. "Well, it is a report they'll never deliver now. Where away, Dave?"

"Home. This town is a jinx. Seems like I can't stick my nose into it without running into a ruckus of some kind."

"You're telling me!" exploded Jumbo. "If this keeps on, I'm going to have the cold shivers every time I think of Boardman's Flat. Think I'll swap places with one of the Pike boys and hole out in that line camp above Painted Rock."

"And yonder, on the right," warned Tonto in a low, curt tone, "we see Luke Converse, looking like he'd just swallowed a rattlesnake. He's heading for us. I hope you boys didn't forget to reload your guns."

It was Converse, all right, and with him was Bob Chehallis and Saugus Lee. They had come out of one of the other saloons and were bearing down on Dave and his companions with open truculence.

"Want a word with you, Salkeld," said Converse harshly. "I understand you've been talkin' fast and loose about me and my boys."

Dave looked at him coldly. A change had taken place in Luke Converse since Dave had seen him last. He looked gaunter, with a sulky worry in his eyes. Evidently things were not going too well with him.

Dave shrugged. "Don't know what you mean, Converse. Make it a little clearer, will you?"

"You're damned right I will!" exploded Converse. "You've been spreading yourself to the effect that you're charging me and my outfit as being responsible for the night raid that was thrown at the sodbusters."

"Whoever told you that, Converse . . . if somebody did tell it to you . . . was lying in their teeth," retorted Dave curtly. "Fact is, I was asked if I thought you were responsible and I said no, I didn't think you were. I still don't think so."

Bob Chehallis spat. "Going mealy-mouthed, eh . . . when your hand is called?"

Jumbo Curtis whimpered like an angry bear: "So that's it! Well, if you got a woolly wolf inside your shirt, Chehallis, turn it loose and let it growl. I'm just in a prime mood right now."

Converse spoke over his shoulder. "Shut up, Bob. I'm doing the talking. Salkeld, I got it straight from a man who was there, that when a flock of sodbusters came down on your outfit charging you with that raid, you turned the blame over on to my crowd."

"And I say again, you heard a damned lie," said Dave coolly. "I'm just wondering if the *hombre* who peddled that lie to you wasn't Zeph Tremper." Dave saw the flicker in Converse's eyes, and laughed curtly. "Thought so. That is just that damned old reptile's caliber. He was the one who first got the settlers to believing the Flying Diamond pulled that raid. When I convinced 'em different . . . and not blaming you, understand . . . he must have run straight to you with that story. I gave you credit for having better sense than to believe that poisonous old whelp, Converse."

"I don't see why he should have bothered, if he hadn't heard you say something," argued Converse stubbornly.

"Ah, hell!" snorted Tonto. "Why waste words on him, Dave? Let him think what he wants and be damned to him."

"No," said Dave mildly. "I don't mind telling him. Listen, Converse, I don't suppose Tremper thought to tell you all the reasons he's got it in for the Flying Diamond, so I'll tell you the latest one. We caught those worthless sons of his cold . . . slow-elking one of our critters. No mistake, understand. I surprised them at the job myself. So some of us dropped in on 'em a little

later . . . they had settled on Cache Creek . . . and invited them
to move on . . . get the hell out. They didn't like that, of course,
but they moved."

Even Converse could see that Dave was speaking the simple
truth, but he still tried to bluster. "I don't know anything about
that. But I do know I'm sick and tired of having every sodbuster
I run across act like he was ready to chuck a slug through me.
I'm going to run down every bit of loose talk I hear of being
thrown at the C Cross and make some of these loose-mouthed
jaspers eat their own damned words."

Dave laughed without any mirth. "So it is finally penetrating
your thick head that the settlers got no love for you, eh? Well,
what did you expect? You've tried to swagger and bull your way
along, like you did back at Stony Ford, and as though you were
the Lord's anointed. And now it has backfired. Well, you got it
coming. I figured you'd find out in time that Gallatin Basin was
just too big for you to get away with that stuff. From what I
hear, you weren't exactly easy-handed with the settlers when
you first hit this basin. Don't cry on my shoulder about it. I got
damned little sympathy for you."

"We're no damned hypocrites," spat Saugus Lee thinly. "We
don't like sodbusters any better than you do, Salkeld . . . but we
ain't so damned spineless we go crawlin' around 'em, lickin'
their boots, just to get along with them."

Jumbo's whimper became a roar of rage. He moved faster
than Dave had ever seen him move before. In one long leap he
was on the sneering Lee and a big fist fell like a post maul. Saugus Lee went down stiffly, knocked cold.

Bob Chehallis blistered a curse and spun on Jumbo, dragging
at a gun. But Jumbo had him before Chehallis could get the
weapon free. He handled Chehallis like a child, jerking the gun
from his fingers, and then belting him with the same lethal fist
that had laid Saugus Lee low. Next he grabbed Luke Converse

by the slack of his shirt and shook the cattleman until his teeth rattled and his eyes bugged out.

"I'm a peaceable man," rumbled Jumbo irately. "But my patience reaches only so far. I been tired of you and your crowd for a long time, Converse. You keep out of the way of the Flying Diamond from here on out, or I'm going to hurt somebody, bad. Now you know!"

When Jumbo let go of him, Converse wobbled around on unsteady legs, mumbling incoherently. Dave caught Jumbo by the arm. "Come on, you wild man," he snapped. "We're getting out of here before you hurt somebody."

Dave steered the mumbling, arm-waving Jumbo to his horse and a moment later the three of them were out of town and spurring along. Tonto's shoulders were shaking and he was giving vent to a series of strangled snorts.

"I'm a peaceable man," wheezed Tonto. "Peaceable . . . and he belts them down like he was driving a corral post. Then he shakes Converse tangle-footed. Oh, yes, says Mister Curtis . . . I'm a peaceable man."

Jumbo glared at him. "Choke away, you old blister. But somebody had to put a stop to their damned gab."

"I'm tired of you," whooped Tonto. "In a minute I'll hurt somebody, says Mister Curtis. Right now I'm just curdling your brains. Next time I'll really hurt you."

"*Aw*," blurted Jumbo in disgust, "aw . . . I hope you choke."

Dave Salkeld grinned tightly, but said nothing. He didn't blame Jumbo. In fact, Jumbo had lost his temper just a split second before Dave's was due to explode. The meeting with Converse had been just another exhibition of Converse's blustering, heavy-mouthed tactics, deliberately staged. The fact that Zeph Tremper had gone to Converse in an attempt to influence him even more strongly against the Flying Diamond was of little importance. What did count was Converse's readiness to grab at any issue, false or true, to start trouble. Stronger than ever was Dave's conviction that at some not very distant time the Flying Diamond and the Cross C were due to fight it out to a finish.

All of Converse's trouble was not in any talk that might be made against him. Converse was unable to find any satisfactory range in Gallatin. He had been forced to realize that his first brag of taking what he wanted on the floor of the basin was an empty one. There were too many settlers for him to handle. It was therefore a reasonable conclusion that Converse would eventually try to take over the range the Flying Diamond was developing on the north fork of Cache Creek.

Riding along, Dave forgot Converse as he swept the misty bulk of the Windy Mountains with narrowed, speculative eyes. Light and shadow showed a tracery of cañons and ridges about the split peak Jim Boardman had pointed out to him. Dave studied those cañons and ridges and into his eyes came a cool gleam and he nodded his head, as though in silent decision.

When they struck Cache Creek and began passing settler camps, they noticed a difference in the attitude of these people. Men hailed them with friendly voices. Women and children tossed shyly waving hands.

"You know," boomed Jumbo, "there was a time when I never thought I'd give a plugged damn what any sodbuster thought of me. But darned if it don't seem pretty good to have 'em act so friendly for a change."

When they reached the Abbott wagon, they found Maidie busily currying the pinto bronco. She had combed and brushed the animal's mane and tail and the pinto shone, sleek and spirited, in the afternoon sun.

"Now all you got to do, Miss Maidie," teased Jumbo, "is to tie a couple of ribbons to that bronc' and it'll be prettied up enough to go to a square dance. Dog-gone! That pinto's hide shines so, it hurts my eyes."

Maidie laughed. "I'm afraid I am a very fickle person. I adored that poor little mare. Yet I'm in love with this rascal already. Dad is away with Sam Olsen again and he said I was to go up to your ranch for the night. So if you gentlemen will wait until I saddle up, I'll ride along with you."

Jumbo was out of his saddle in a flash. "I'll dress that bronc' for you." He caught up Maidie's saddle and blanket and advanced upon the pinto with exaggerated caution. "Now, looky here, you wall-eyed, piebald chunk of ugly cussedness, don't you take a cut at me with either end of your bony carcass. If you do, I'll knot your straggle tail plenty."

"For shame!" Maidie laughed. "Serve you right if Sunbeam did kick you a couple, after all that slander."

Jumbo stared at her, pop-eyed. "Huh! Did I hear you call this bronc' . . . Sunbeam?"

Dave chuckled. "Get that saddle on, you big ape. Don't keep the lady waiting."

As they started out, Maidie looked with sober eyes at Tonto's bandaged hand. "There's been some kind of trouble," she said. "You didn't have anything wrong with your hand when you started for town. What happened?"

"Just a little ruckus with a couple of those whelps who raided the basin last night," said Tonto briefly. "Don't amount to a thing."

Maidie exclaimed excitedly: "You mean you ran into some of those raiders in town?"

"Two of them."

"What did they have to say for themselves?"

"They started talking with lead . . . and got answered the same way," answered Tonto briefly.

"Oh." Maidie's eyes grew wide and startled. Her glance

flickered from one to another of the three men she rode with. She asked no more questions.

CHAPTER SIXTEEN

Gallatin Basin lay still and vast and dark under the pale stars. Dave Salkeld, at the head of ten riders, worked south along the foothills of the Windy Mountains. When the black bulk of the split peak rose on his left, Dave reined in and twisted in his saddle.

"Maybe we're having this night ride for nothing, boys," he said. "But I don't think we are. It's reasonable to believe that those raiders will hit the basin again tonight. Right now the settlers are stampeded and disorganized and easy prey. But before long they'll be organized and far too tough for that raiding gang to handle. Therefore it is common sense to figure that they'll keep on hitting and hitting as many times as they can before that organization is an actual fact. From what Boardman said today, that raid on his pack train took place in a cañon somewhere under that split peak up yonder. I believe the same outfit raided that pack train as hit the basin. Chances are they got a hide-out camp somewhere back around the peak. I'm playing my cards on the gamble that they'll work in and out of the mountains through the cañon that comes down from the north side of the peak. Jumbo, I'm giving you four men. I want you to sift back through the timber until you hit the mouth of that cañon. When you get there, hide out and watch. If riders come out, let 'em come. Me and the other boys will be waiting for them. I think we can surprise 'em, cut 'em up pretty bad. They'll light back for their hide-out. You'll catch 'em when they're panicky. Then . . . give 'em hell. Savvy?"

"Plenty," growled Jumbo. "The chore will be a pleasure."

"All right. These men go with Jumbo." Dave called off four names and the riders swung silently away to follow Jumbo, who was already heading into the timber.

When the last sound of the departing horses had vanished, Dave swung off to the right and rode slowly, looking the country over under the thin starlight. He chose his ambuscade carefully, where the timber thinned out to a narrow stretch of open country, with another thin fringe of timber on the basin side. It was in this lower timber that Dave reined in and dismounted.

"We'll bunch the horses on the lower side of this timber," he directed, "then go back on foot to watch that open stretch. If we can scatter 'em and bust 'em up first, we'll hit leather later to run 'em down."

He scattered his men through the timber, close to the edge of the clear space. Dirk was on the extreme right end of the line, Pudge on the left. Dave kept Wampus close to him, for Wampus was the youngest and inexperienced at this sort of thing. The other two were Bill Shore and Ike Caveny.

Silence settled down. A soft wind came down from the mountains, stirring the timber to vague rustlings. "Those coyotes may ride plumb to one side of us, Dave," murmured Wampus. "This is a big country."

"They might," acknowledged Dave. "I've figured that, too. If they do, and get behind us and into the basin, we'll hear the first shooting that starts. And then we'll collect Jumbo and the other boys and do our damnedest to get between them and their retreat. And they won't find the basin as easy pickings as it was last night. I'll bet there ain't a settler in the basin who won't sleep awful light tonight, and they'll all have guns right under their hands. They haven't had time to organize in a mass. But a one-man organization, hid out under a wagon, with a gun ready to roll, ain't the easiest proposition to handle, even with the odds all against him."

"Suppose they do come out this way, like you figure?" asked Wampus. "How you going to identify them in the dark? How will you know they ain't just a bunch of peaceful jaspers drifting into the basin?"

Dave grinned tightly. "They'll identify themselves quick enough."

"I hope so," sighed Wampus. "Me, I'm plenty anxious to brand a few coyotes, but I'd hate like the devil to cut down on some innocent jigger."

"Innocent jiggers won't be prowling down out of those mountains at this time of night. Now take it easy and don't get restless. We may have to wait only a little while before we draw something. Again, we may have to wait all night and not start a thing."

The Flying Diamond contingent had not left headquarters until around 9:00 p.m. By the time they were set and waiting, it was nearly 11:00. Midnight came and passed without an untoward sound to break the majestic silence of the sleeping mountains. Coyotes wailed in the far distance. Once Dave thought he caught an echo of the deep, hoarse howl of a loafer wolf somewhere up on the mountain slope, and he made a mental note to have Boardman bring in half a dozen wolf traps, to be used when the winter snows drove the four-footed calf killers down from the higher ranges.

Beside him, Dave heard a soft snore. He grinned. Wampus was a great kid. Eager, willing, full of boyish enthusiasm for every job he tackled. Already a top hand when in the saddle and with a rope in his hand, he was totally unseasoned for the kind of job that might lie ahead. This was the reason he had kept the curly-topped kid beside him.

The lateness of the hour was not dismaying to Dave, nor

making him yet doubtful that he had guessed wrong concerning the intentions of the raiders or the route they would use coming out of the mountains. For it was the hours of the very early morning when men slept soundly, when their thoughts were confused, and when they were the easiest prey to strike.

Dave peered up through the thick tracery of foliage overhead, catching some idea of the wheel of the stars. Dawn wouldn't come for at least three hours yet. Plenty of time for the raiders to show, to strike, to get back to their hideaway again.

He started to shift his position to ease his cramped muscles. At that moment he heard the faint *clink* of a hoof striking a stone. Instantly all vestige of drowsiness left him. He strained eager eyes across the open space above, where the dim starlight laid a pale glow.

Now he saw them, a dark mass of riders breaking out of the gloom of the upper timber, coming straight across the opening. They came on at a walk, as though they would ride right over him. But suddenly they stopped. A harsh voice carried clearly through the still, heavy air.

"We split up as arranged in camp. Estes and his crowd go south. I take my gang north. If Hawkhurst and Costain had come back, we'd have some idea how the settlers were lined up. But they didn't. Nobody knows why. If they got drunk on us, they'd better not ever come back, for I'll take their hides off with a quirt. As it is, we got to go it blind. Chances are the sodbusters will be more or less on the look-out. Which means we got to go at them a little different. When a wagon is located, two men go in quiet and on foot. If the sodbuster is on guard, Injun up on him and knock him on the head. Then call in the others. Six wagons by each gang will bring a good profit, and we'll have that much time. If any damned hoe man has got his poke hid out, make him tell you where it is if you have to slice off his ears. All right, get going!"

160

Dave did not wait any longer. He lifted his saddle gun, and at the same time kicked the sleeping Wampus on the leg. And then, straight into the black mass of men and horses, Dave began levering shot after shot.

The thin snarl of the rifle ripped across the flank of the mountains, raising echoes of flat thunder. Hardly had the first shot gone than Pudge and Dirk, Bill Shore and Ike Caveny opened up.

The first result was terrific. The black bulk of the raiders was a cursing, tangled shambles. Men and horses went down under the criss-crossing hail of lead.

Wampus, jerked from his slumber by Dave's kick and the crashing gunfire right beside him, lunged up stupidly.

At that moment, free of the first stunning surprise, the raiders began to scatter out and return the fire. Almost with the first return shot, Dave heard Wampus give a gasp, then a thin, whimpering moan. Wampus—the curly-headed kid was down!

Something cold and tragic and bleak ran through Dave Salkeld. There was nothing he could do for the kid at the moment. For the raiders, under roaring, cursing orders, were scattering wide and beginning to lace that lower timber with lead. But Dave knew what had happened. It was a shot thrown at the flame of his gun that had gone wide from him but had hit Wampus. His fault. He should have awakened the kid when he heard the first sound of the raiders' approach. There was only one thing to do now. That was to pick targets and even up as much as he could for Wampus.

But those targets were individual riders now, flitting back across the open through the faint starlight, and those targets were shooting back. Lead whipping above Dave's head showered him with twigs and bits of battered bark, slashed from the trees.

Dave picked a target and fired three fast shots. The third one did the trick. The horse still galloped crazily about, but the saddle it carried was empty. Dave plugged fresh loads through the loading gate of his weapon, while his stabbing eyes searched for a new target.

There weren't many left. Most of those still able to ride after that first terrific fusillade had cut back for the shelter of the timber. But leathery old Bill Shore was poison with a saddle gun, in daylight or dark, and he had piled up two men and a horse while the raiders scattered.

The survivors of the ambush were safely back in the upper timber by now. Dave could hear them yelling back and forth. But there was that one hoarse voice of authority that shouted them down. With no target to show, Dave got to one knee and levered his gun dry again, searching the black line of timber above. And his four faithful ones, taking the cue, did the same.

The raiders had been too completely surprised, too wickedly punished to do more than throw frantic and desperate lead while getting out of the fatal opening and back into the security of the upper timber. Once there, they soon quit shooting and retreated swiftly toward the fastnesses of the north cañon. They had no idea how many men made up that deadly ambuscade, nor who those men were. They only knew that they had been surprised as they had plotted to surprise others, and that their ranks had been decimated heavily. The survivors fled for sanctuary.

All shooting died and Dave Salkeld's thin line of valiants closed in for further instruction. They found Dave carrying Wampus out into the starlight where he might see a little better. Wampus hung limply, arms and legs and head. But, although shot through the body, the young cowboy was not dead.

"Don't tell me the kid is . . . is done for, Dave," burst out Dirk harshly. "Not . . . not Wampus?"

"He's still alive," said Dave bleakly. "But for how long . . . I don't know. We got to get him to headquarters. Here, give me a hand. We got to stop this bleeding. Pudge, fork leather and hit for town. Roust that doctor out and get him to headquarters if you have to use a gun on him. Git!"   —

Pudge hurried off. While Dirk helped Dave with Wampus, Bill Shore and Ike Caveny prowled out into the open, to look over the battlefield. It was at this moment that a burst of gunfire, muted by distance, carried down out of the cañon. It rattled along for the space of a minute, then died away.

"Jumbo and the other boys," said Dave curtly. "They've got in their licks. We gave those damned raiders something to think about this night. We'll have to get his shirt off, Dirk. Easy, now."

By the time Dave and Dirk had gotten rude bandages on Wampus's wound, Bill Shore and Ike Caveny came back.

"Seven," reported Bill succinctly. "Seven men and nine horses. Reckon those polecats will think and think long before they hit this basin again. And did you hear what that *hombre* with the big voice said about Injuning up on the wagons? This little soirée saved the lives of maybe a dozen sodbusters tonight. And it sounds like Jumbo and the other boys might have grabbed off a few bites themselves."

"No matter how many sodbusters we saved, we'll have paid a stiff price if Wampus . . . if Wampus dies," said Dirk fiercely through set teeth. "We'll have to make a blanket litter, Dave."

"I'll get the bronc's," said Ike Caveny, hurrying off.

They had the horses there and were trying to figure the litter out, when they heard a hail from the upper timber. It was Jumbo's voice. Bill Shore answered, and Jumbo, with four riders following him, rode down across the open. But one of those riders was not upright in his saddle. Instead, he was jackknifed across it.

"We got four of 'em," reported Jumbo grimly. "But . . . we lost Tobe Severn. One of those devils shore was a hellcat with a gun. He got Tobe and broke right by us. The whelp seemed to have a charmed life. I had three shots at him myself and never got a feather. Who . . . who . . . say, don't tell me that's Wampus, the kid?" Jumbo scrambled from his saddle, dropped on one knee. "Not dead," he said, a sort of flat relief in his big voice. "How bad is he, Dave?"

"Pretty bad. We're figuring out a litter to get him to headquarters. Pudge has gone to town after the doctor."

"Litter, be damned!" exploded Jumbo. "This way will be quicker. Hand him up to me."

Jumbo went back into his saddle, held out his big arms.

"You can't carry him all the way home," argued Dave. "Wampus ain't a baby. He's a grown man."

"I can carry him plumb across a wide state, if it means his chance for life," growled Jumbo. "Hand him up!"

So they lifted Wampus carefully, until Jumbo got his powerful arms under him. "All right," said Jumbo. "Let's go."

They were silent on the way home. Their mission had been highly successful, more successful than Dave had hoped for, even in his most optimistic moment. But they had paid a price. One good comrade was making his last ride, tied across his own saddle. It was problematical whether Jumbo would have a live or dead man in his arms when they reached headquarters.

Dawn caught them before they got home and its cold grayness was symbolic of their feelings. Dave glanced at Jumbo and his burden. Wampus was limp and still, his curly head hanging over Jumbo's arm. A deep pallor underlay the normal tan of Wampus's face.

Jumbo's jaw was set, little ridges of muscle showing along the angles. His lips were tightly pressed.

"You're catchin' hell, big feller," said Dave gravely. "You shouldn't have tried to carry him so far alone. Swing him over to me. I'll carry him for a while."

"And maybe start him bleeding again," growled Jumbo.

"Nothin' doing. I'll make it."

Jumbo did make it. They reached headquarters just as the sun lifted into sight. Buck Custer, Mose, Maidie Abbott, Tonto, and Jim Abbott came hurrying out of the cook shack. Maidie gave a little cry, her face going white. "He . . . he's not dead?"

"No," gritted Jumbo. "He looks it, but he ain't. I can tell. Mose, come here and take him."

Jumbo made a last effort as he swung Wampus out and into Mose's ready arms. Mose was mumbling softly: "Jes' a curly-haided kid, this Wampus boy. Jes' a curly haid. But ol' Mose'll take care of him. Li'l Missy, yo' quick git me some hot water and clean cloth. We take care of this boy, yo' and Mose."

Jumbo, free of his burden, sagged forward in the saddle, his arms hanging stiffly and knotted by his sides. Dave and the rest pulled him out of the saddle and found they had to hold him up. A tight, thin grin touched Jumbo's lips. "Sorry, boys," he mumbled. "I feel sort of done in. I'll be all right in a minute."

"You big, dumb, strong-backed ox," berated Dirk huskily. "All you did was pack a hundred-and-sixty-pound man a good ten miles and now you're all fagged out. You big sissy!"

They got Jumbo into the bunkhouse and laid him down. They yanked his shirt off and fell to rubbing and flexing his big, tension-knotted arms and shoulders, while Jumbo writhed and cursed softly at the torment of returning circulation.

Presently he swept them aside and got to his feet. "All right now," he said. "Ain't Pudge got here with that doctor yet?"

"Coming now," said Tonto, who stood in the bunkhouse door. "Jumbo, I've cussed your clumsy soul more than once. I may again. But right now I'm telling the world you're all man."

CHAPTER SEVENTEEN

Back in the wild depths of the mountains, six men gathered at a campground. Wolf Rossiter, a dirty neckerchief tied about his head, marched up and down, raging with hoarse, wild curses. Lon Estes, his thin face a gray mask of fury, his eyes bleak and deadly, stood staring out into the distance.

"Hawkhurst and Costain sold us out!" yelled Rossiter. "They sold us out and let us ride right into an ambush. They must have tipped those damned sodbusters off and told 'em where to look for us. The dirty, double-crossing. . . ." Rossiter went into another volley of cursing.

Estes's voice sounded like a whiplash. "Shut up! Shut up that damned bawling around. It's your own fault . . . all of this. I tried to show you sense . . . but it didn't get over. I tell you it's all your own fault."

Rossiter turned on him, his curses vicious. It was plain that the renegade leader was half crazy with rage. His hands began to fan back and forth past the gun butts at his hips, hands set like claws.

"That'll be all out of you, Estes," he blurted. "I don't want any more of your damned second guessing. In a minute. . . ."

"You'll shut up!" rapped Estes thinly. His hand flickered and Rossiter found himself looking into a gun. "From here on out, you don't have much to say. I'm running what's left of this gang now. If you don't think so, take a look at the boys."

Rossiter looked, saw the remaining four renegades drawing

166

up beside Estes. "You're not smart enough, Rossiter," went on the gunman. "You led the gang into something that near wiped all of us out. Eleven men we left back there on the foothills, Rossiter. And it was your fault. We that are left have picked a new leader. That's me. From now on, you take orders, not give 'em. If you don't like it, you can ride away. But your health won't be good if you quit us."

It was a savagely bitter pill for Rossiter to swallow. Yet it was the law of any outlaw pack. His leadership would stand only as long as he could hold it. Even in his bitter fury, Rossiter could see that his time as leader was past.

"All right," he snarled, "if you think you can do a better job. But Hawkhurst and Costain. . . ."

"Forget those two," said Estes harshly. "It wasn't their fault. They must have run into something in Boardman's Flat. That's why they didn't come back. They never sold us out. There was nothing they could gain by doing a thing of that sort. I tell you it was all your own fault. You would raid that pack train to get some cheap grub. I warned you not to, as it would be a giveaway as to where we were holed up. And those weren't a flock of sodbusters who set that ambush. Sodbusters don't shoot that good. Those *hombres* were cowhands. My guess is the Flying Diamond bunch."

"The Flying Diamond!" snarled Rossiter. "But how . . . why?"

"Your particular kind of a fool never gives the other side credit for having any savvy," cut in Estes. "That Salkeld *hombre* . . . I hate his guts . . . and, if it's the last thing I ever do, I'll see the day with him going down under my smoke. Yet . . . he's nobody's fool. You admit one man got away from that pack train. He carried word to Boardman. The news would soon get out. It served to show where we were hanging out. I told you to cut south through the mountains before breaking out into the basin on this second raid. But no. You would have it your own way. You went down this north cañon and Salkeld had it figured we'd come out that way. You know now what happened. Yes, Rossiter, you're a fool. And me and these other boys . . . we don't want to have a fool telling us what to do any longer. Now the choice is up to you. You can ride as just one of the gang, taking orders from me. Or. . . ." Estes tilted his gun suggestively.

Rossiter looked over the men facing him. He saw nothing but cold and watchful hostility in their faces. He swallowed thickly. "All right. I'll stick. But there's only six of us left. What can we do?"

"Coming back from that free-for-all murder down in the foothills, I've been thinking of what we'll do," said Estes, sliding his gun back into the leather. "We're going to have a little talk with Converse."

"Converse? What good will that do?"

"Converse has been out of luck finding range for his herd. I know that *hombre*. He'd like nothing better than to grab off that Flying Diamond range. Right now I think he'll be willing to make a deal. If he doesn't, he stands to lose his shirt. And Converse is the sort to have big ideas. Once he gets hold of the Flying Diamond, he'll start spreading down into the basin as much as he can. We'll get in our licks there. It's worth the try. Come on, we ride."

The first gray light of dawn was breaking when the remaining outlaws, with Lon Estes as their new leader, came up to the Cross C camp. The cook was just stirring when, out of the dawn mists, the bittered-eyed figure of Lon Estes confronted him. The cook gulped, startled.

"Keep your shirt on, *amigo*," said Estes curtly. "We come friendly. We want to have a talk with Converse. Roust him out, will you?"

While the cook hurried off, Estes looked over the camp with

coldly calculating eyes. There were signs here that his eye did not miss. It was plain that the Cross C outfit was more or less demoralized. No guards had been set for the night. On the way in Estes and his companions had passed a lot of Cross C cattle and there were no night hawks riding to make sure that neither rustlers or slow-elkers got in any shady licks. Estes knew the reason.

From the time the Cross C had hit Gallatin Basin it had been continually on the move, from here to there, unable to find a satisfactory place to land and stay put. This uncertainty was bound to affect the morale of the crew. They might even be losing confidence in Converse's leadership. All of which suited Estes right down to the ground. It meant that the Cross C crew would be more than willing to listen to his ideas. And even Converse, growing desperate over the stalemate he was in, would lend a receptive ear. Estes murmured a warning to the men behind him.

"Remember, I do all the talking."

The cook returned, followed by a sleep-muddled Luke Converse, who stared at Estes and the other renegades suspiciously. "What do you want?" he mumbled. "What's the idea getting a man out of his blankets this time of morning?"

"Business," said Estes crisply. "That means money to you and satisfaction to me. Interested?"

Converse hesitated. Then he shrugged. "Won't do no harm to listen, I reckon. Light down and rest your saddles. Soup, get that fire going."

The cook hurried about and soon a ruddy blaze was crackling. Estes and his men gathered about it, and Converse stood, feet spread, sucking on a cigarette. "Shoot!" he growled.

"I hate a man," said Estes. "I hate him so bad, I'll never rest until I see him dead on the ground in front of me. That man is Dave Salkeld."

Converse stirred, drawing a quick breath. "You don't hate him any worse than I do. Go on."

"You're in a tough spot, ain't you, Converse? You got a herd of cattle and no good range to put 'em on. The sodbusters got you shut out of the basin proper and the Flying Diamond has got the only real piece of range back here in the hills. How'd you like to take over that Flying Diamond range . . . and the herd along with it?"

Estes, watching closely, saw Converse's knuckles grow white as he clenched his fists. "I'd give ten years of my life to do just that," he growled hoarsely. "Yeah, ten years of my life."

"Then I guess we can get together," purred Estes. "Things have been breaking pretty smooth for the Flying Diamond. Too smooth for their own good. They're beginning to feel fat and sassy and well satisfied with themselves. Which makes them just ripe to be pushed over, providing we hit 'em at the right time. Will your men follow you, Converse . . . on a night raid on the Flying Diamond?"

"Will they? Hell, they been trying to talk me into such a thing for the past week. I've been playing with the idea myself, but holding off until the set-up is just right. You think it could be done, then?"

"I know it could," snapped Estes. "Hell, they're mortal men. Lead can smash them down, same as anyone else. And with the element of surprise on our side, we can smash them flat. Only we don't want to put the idea off too long, else they may get wise to us."

Converse was intrigued, mightily so. This showed in the dull glow of his eyes, the restless shift of them. Now he looked straight at Estes. "Believing that you hate Salkeld as you say you do . . . still, I can't figure just that behind your idea. What's the rest of it?"

Estes took a chance. He had to. "You may have heard of a

night raid on the sodbusters a few nights ago, Converse. Well. . . ."

Converse stared. Then he laughed harshly. "So! You fellers were responsible, eh? Well, that's all right with me. I hate any sodbuster . . . all sodbusters. If you can put such a fear in them they'll all get out of Gallatin, that'll suit me fine. Give me just that much more range."

"Exactly," said Estes swiftly. "There is only one solid organized fighting force in this basin. That is the Flying Diamond. We bust that outfit and we got the basin at our mercy. You'll get fat off the set-up and so will we. You can have the cattle and the range, as long as we can have the settlers . . . and their pokes."

Converse slammed a clenched fist into an open palm. "It's a deal!" he exclaimed. "With you fellers riding with us, we'll have the Flying Diamond outmanned nearly two to one. When do we strike?"

Estes flashed a triumphant glance at Wolf Rossiter. "The sooner the better, I figure. Now we can get down to real planning. How about some grub?"

Chapter Eighteen

The doctor came out of the Flying Diamond bunkhouse, scrubbing his hands with a wet towel. To Dave Salkeld's unspoken question, the doctor shrugged. "Maybe . . . maybe not," he said. "Hard telling yet. He's young, and a clean-lived youngster. Those kind can make recoveries that defy all medical science. The fact that he is still alive is a big argument in his favor. I can make a better guess twelve hours from now. Having the girl here to nurse him is a big help, too. All we can do is keep him quiet . . . and hope. I'd like to stay right here with him until the crisis is past. I can't do it. There's a settler's wife in town due to hand me a baby any time. I'll try and get back tomorrow."

Jim Abbott prepared to leave, also. "I'm going to see that this basin hears of what you boys have done for it, Dave," he said. "I think, when the word of this gets out, you and your boys can figure on more friends than you ever had before."

There was an unpleasant chore to be done. They wrapped Tobe Severn in blankets and carried him up to Painted Rock. There they dug the grave and buried him, with the everlasting rock as his headstone. Then they returned to headquarters and went soberly and grimly about their daily work.

Dave Salkeld went into the bunkhouse softly. Beside Wampus's bunk sat Maidie Abbott. Dave touched her on the shoulder. "You better go rest," he murmured. "I'll sit with him for a while."

She shook her head. "I'm not tired. Oh, Dave . . . when is

Gallatin Basin really going to become what it appears to be, a peaceful, beautiful place for people to live in?"

"When certain elements are stamped out," answered Dave. "Not until then. It has always been this way, I reckon. Every new territory that men move in to conquer has its period of lawlessness, of robbery, brutality, and murder. In time, better men organize and bring in law and order. It will be the same here."

"But . . . but always there is a price to pay," said Maidie. "Like . . . like Wampus here . . . and Tobe Severn. Dave . . . was Lon Estes one of that raiding crew?"

Dave nodded gravely. "I heard him called by name, when the head of the raiders was giving last instructions. I'm sorry, Maidie."

She looked at him. "Dad and I were fools, Dave . . . for ever picking him up. It is just as though we picked up a rattlesnake and nursed it back to health. I wish"—she ended a little fiercely—"we'd left him where he was to die. It would have been better, that way."

Dave studied her gravely. There was an intriguing gallantry in the way she carried her curly head. The line of her partially averted face was soft, sweetly curved—a little sad.

The day moved slowly on. All sounds of industry about the Flying Diamond were muted. From time to time, various members of the crew came tiptoeing softly, for a report on Wampus, who lay very still, eyes closed, his face a gray pallor under his suntan. Jumbo stared at the curly-headed kid, gulped, and went out a little blindly. Maidie had to blink hard to keep back the tears when she saw that. Yet a little later, when she felt of the wounded rider's pulse, she found it faintly stronger than before.

Mose came in, his eyes round and solemn, with none of the usual merriment in them. When Maidie whispered to the old

Negro that Wampus seemed to be getting back a little strength, Mose almost blubbered.

"Glory be," he mumbled. "I'se goin' back to my kitchen an' pray like I ain't prayed since I was a li'l pickaninny. We just cain't let that curly-haid die, li'l Missy."

He patted Maidie on the shoulder and went out.

Dave, restless and on edge, saddled a bronco and rode up past Painted Rock and into the little basin above, for a visit with the Pike boys. They reported everything quiet, so far. Dave told them about the battle with the raiders, of the smashing victory, and their own casualties.

"Tobe Severn was a good man," said Jerry Pike gravely. "But that is one of the chances of life. I'm hoping that kid, Wampus, makes the grade. Smashing that raiding gang ought to put the outfit in strong with the settlers, Dave."

"It will make us plenty of friends, all right. But we still got some enemies running loose, Jerry. Lon Estes, that gunfighter, was with those raiders, and we didn't find him among the casualties. Something tells me we haven't seen the last of him."

As Dave was preparing to leave, Ed Pike said: "We heard a loafer wolf howling a couple of times, back up in the timber. If you could get hold of a few traps, Dave, we'll make a try at getting that four-footed devil before it starts working on some of our calves."

"I'll do that, Ed. I'll put in an order with Boardman this afternoon. Number four ought to be about the right size."

"Number fours will hold him. Get half a dozen."

Dave rode back to headquarters, insisted on Maidie getting some rest, detailed Mose to take her place for a few hours, then headed for Boardman's Flat in company with Jumbo and Buck Custer.

Down on the main branch of Cache Creek they saw no sign of Jim Abbott or Sam Olsen, but Mrs. Olsen, a statuesque, wholesome-looking woman with a wonderful crown of yellow hair, told them why.

"Sam and Mister Abbott have gone to town. They left about an hour ago. They got word that those Trempers were caught stealing from some wagons. They're holding a trial in town. The messenger who brought the news said it looked like a lynching." She twisted her hands nervously and asked almost the same question Maidie Abbott had asked Dave earlier that day. "Why must such a beautiful country as this cost so much in violence and death and bloodshed?"

"I reckon, ma'am," said Buck Custer gravely, "it's the price set by fate. It is always the same."

When they reached town, they found it seething with excitement. Word had reached far into the basin and settlers jammed the street. Dave and his companions found that the trial was being held in the Free Land Saloon. They also found that they did not have a chance of getting into the place. It was packed to suffocation, not another inch of standing room available.

Staring at the close-packed crowd about the door of the place, trying to get a word of what was going on inside, Dave nodded grimly. "It's here," he said. "And a good thing."

"What's here?" asked Jumbo.

"The beginning of law and order. It's come quicker than usual, but I reckon events have forced it. Well, no use us standing here with our feet in our mouths, waiting to hear the verdict. It'll be spread fast enough, once it's given. I've got to see Bill Boardman."

They found Boardman alone. All interest in the town centered at the Free Land Saloon at the moment. Boardman shook hands heartily. "You boys made a name for yourselves last night," he said. "I reckon I owe you some thanks myself, for I don't have any doubt but that it was the same crowd who robbed my pack train. Some of the boys rode out to the

175

battlefield, and, from what they told me, you shore put a crimp in that gang of renegades. Now if those settlers will just hang that Tremper crowd, maybe decent men will have a chance to draw a long breath."

"Before I forget, Bill . . . on your next order from Aspen City, bring me in half a dozen number four Newhouse traps. There's a loafer wolf hanging out around our herd and the quicker we get the brute, the more calves we save."

Boardman nodded and made a note of the order.

"What's the story behind this Tremper trouble?" asked Buck Custer.

Boardman shrugged. "Just plain damn' dirty thievery, I reckon. They were caught red-handed, looting some wagons. It seems half a dozen settlers had bunched together to help each other haul timber and build cabins. They came back in a bunch and found the Trempers going through a wagon. The Trempers were acting pretty rough with the wife of one of the settlers. The Trempers were surprised and didn't have a chance to put up any fight. Some of the settlers wanted to shoot the Trempers right then and there, but some cooler heads talked 'em out of it, saying that here was a chance to weld the settlers together and start a real law-and-order movement. They tied the Tremper crowd up and brought 'em to town, sending out word that they'd be tried all legal and according to Hoyle." Boardman grinned. "I don't know how legal it'll be, but I reckon it is a step in the right direction."

A wild yell echoed from the street. Dave reached the door of the trading post first. Settlers were pouring out of the Free Land Saloon, some jubilant and raucous with excitement, others grim and stern of face. Among the latter were Jim Abbott, Sam Olsen, and Stinson.

Then the Trempers appeared, father and three sons. Their hands were tied behind them. They shambled as they walked, a great and ghastly fear in their faces. They were started toward the outskirts of town, where stood a little grove of gaunt cottonwoods. Already men had run ahead and tossed four noosed ropes over gnarled but staunch limbs. The crowd massed about the trees, hiding the doomed men from sight.

The crowd grew quiet and Dave could hear the echo of Dan Stinson's deep voice. Then came a brief surge of action. The ropes grew taut. Dave turned away, building a cigarette. A deep and gusty breath seemed to come from the crowd. A drunk yelled crazily.

"Watch 'em kick! Watch 'em . . . !"

He broke off abruptly as Jim Abbott's fist crashed into his jaw, knocking him sprawling.

The crowd began to break up. All the signs were there. Law and order were in the saddle. The first page of the book had been written there, under the afternoon sun. A breeze rippled the leaves of the cottonwoods. Four still figures spun slowly. . . .

When Dave and Buck and Jumbo rode out of town an hour later, there were no signs. The cottonwoods were as they had been before man, clamoring after his destiny, had ever set foot in Gallatin Basin. But in the town's boothill—men were laboring with pick and shovel.

Man, thought Dave somberly, *built his own destiny, but always at heavy cost. Fear, anger, hatred. Greed, cruelty, death. But later came the majesty of lasting achievement.*

Suddenly he was weary, weary of fight and struggle. His thoughts took a strange turn. He saw Maidie Abbott, her curly head high, her smile soft and gallant. She would be standing in the doorway of a ranch house, watching for him, her smile one of welcome, tired but content from long days of worthwhile work. Together they might build a future.

He shook his head. His thoughts were getting away from

him, running thus to more gentle things. This basin had not been subdued. This virgin land was far from conquered. A wild savage land, where wild savage men still rode. The first page of the book had been written, true enough. But there were many other pages ahead. And wasn't he taking much for granted? Maidie was friendly and real with him, but he had no right to build that friendliness into something richer, more enduring. Not yet, anyhow. He was being an egotistical fool and somehow felt that he owed Maidie Abbott an apology. He murmured it, a silent one.

The sun was setting when Dave went softly into the bunkhouse. Mose looked at him with exultant eyes and his infectious grin. "Look, Marse Dave," he said. "Look at that curly-haid' boy. He done get a li'l color back. He gwine git stronger every minute."

Wampus did look better. That gray, still pallor was not nearly so marked. In its place was a hint of real color. Dave's first thought was of fever, but when he laid a careful hand on Wampus's forehead, he found it safely cool.

Dave nodded. "You go along and get supper, Mose. I'll stay with him now."

As purple dusk settled down, Maidie came in looking bright and rested. Her eyes were shining as she looked at Wampus. "He's better, Dave. He's better."

"Yes . . . he's better. If we get him through tonight, I'll feel we've won the fight."

It was a long, long night. Dave had had little rest in the past twenty-four hours, but he refused to leave the side of Wampus. Maidie sat with him. They both knew the tough time. From midnight on. That was the hurdle. The death hours.

They saw Wampus go a long way down into the shadows. They saw the newly gained color fade and fade and the pallor come back. And there wasn't a thing they could do. The doctor would have helped mightily. But the doctor could not be two places at once. Somewhere he was bringing a new life into the world. Here it was touch and go, whether one life would leave as the other entered.

Maidie took one of the wounded cowboy's hands in both of hers, as though she would warm it and through it transmit some of her own abounding vitality. Dave fixed his eye on a tiny pulse in Wampus's throat and watched it stoically.

Outside, from time to time, would come the sound of a man clearing his throat, and drifting in through the open doorway would come the faint tang of cigarette smoke. The whole outfit was standing by, giving silent aid to Wampus on his most perilous ride.

That pulse grew fainter and fainter to a certain point, then clung there tenaciously. Dave saw tears stealing down Maidie's cheeks and he put an arm about her. Her lips were moving and very softly Dave heard the words of an old, almost forgotten childhood prayer.

Gray dawn came stealing almost before Dave realized it. Then suddenly he was aware that that precious pulse had grown quiet and strong and full, that Wampus no longer looked shrunken and queerly wasted. Substance had come back to him in some wonderful manner, substance and strength. For the tousled, curly head turned on the pillow and Wampus sighed deeply, like a child sleeping.

Dave went outside, almost staggering in his fatigue. They were all out there, Buck, Jumbo, Pudge, Dirk, and Mose. Their eyes fixed anxiously on his face. Dave smiled.

"You can go sleep now, boys," he said. "The stout rascal made it. Wampus ain't going to leave us. He's made the grade."

Jumbo whooped softly as he stood erect and stretched his big arms. "Sleep," he rumbled. "Who wants to sleep? Show me a job . . . a tough job. Right now I could push a mountain over.

Mose, you black hellion, how about some breakfast?"

Mose scuttled for the cook shack, his big grin back, eyes and teeth shining.

Buck Custer took Dave by the arm. "You're going to sleep, Dave," he said gruffly. "You've gone long enough without it. Get in there on a bunk and get some rest. And Maidie, she's got to do the same. Tonto and me, we've had plenty of chance to sleep. We take over now."

"All right," said Dave. "If you can get Maidie to rest, too."

"I'll handle her," promised Buck.

He did. He picked her up bodily and tossed her onto a vacant bunk. "No argument," he said, gruffly gentle. "Sleep you need . . . sleep you get."

She smiled and burrowed her head into the pillow.

It was late in the afternoon when Dave Salkeld awakened. Maidie still slept, curly hair spread on the pillow. Someone had thrown a light blanket over her. Her cheek was pink and dewy with sleep, her breathing soft and regular. She looked very young, very winsome.

Mose sat beside Wampus, gently bathing the young rider's face, all the while softly crooning an old spiritual. As Dave moved up beside him, Mose looked up, grinning. "Curly-haid coming along. He's gwine live, sho' nuff."

When Dave went out, it was to see Jim Abbott riding up. "How's Wampus?" asked the bearded settler as he began unsaddling.

"Over the hump," said Dave. "Maidie's been swell, Jim. I think she had as much to do with the kid's condition as the doc did. We finally got her to rest. She's still sleeping. Looks like you've lost a daughter . . . at least until she figures Wampus is well enough again to do without nursing."

"Suits me," said Abbott in satisfaction. "I hope she can stay here with you boys until things get good and quiet again in this basin. I know she's safe here. And if she was down at my place, I'd be worried all the time about her. I'm not forgetting that damned wolf of a Lon Estes is still running loose. Dave, I wish now I'd drove the wagon over him, instead of picking him up, that time we found him."

"I expect a few more doses of the rope, such as was handed out to the Trempers, will tone this basin down a lot, Jim. The law-and-order idea travels fast, once it gets away to a start."

"It sure was overdue on that worthless crowd," said Abbott grimly. "And if Estes had been included, I'd feel better yet."

Supper, that evening, was an affair of almost gaiety. Knowledge that Wampus, the curly-headed kid of the outfit, was out of the shadows, gave a fillip to the spirits of everyone. Maidie had awakened and she sat beside her father, bright of eye, rosy of cheek, and she laughed more than once at the drawling foolishness that Jumbo and Dirk and Pudge traded back and forth. Buck Custer had elected to stay with Wampus while the rest ate, so Mose was free to take care of his regular duties, and he shuffled back and forth from the kitchen, grinning and chuckling to himself.

His meal over with, Dave left the rest to sit about the table for a time, while he sauntered down along the corrals alone. The cool, descending freshness of the night laid invigorating fingers on his throat and the lean planes of his face. The stars hung softly and luminously. Something swelled in Dave's breast. This country, new and vigorous, was worth fighting for, worth everything it cost a man to win and hold it. None of the big prizes of life came easy. All of them meant toil and danger and hardship. But the rewards were big, big.

He built a cigarette and savored the tang of the smoke with a keen relish. Not so long ago, this whole set-up had been only a dream that he and Buck Custer had had. Then it had seemed

181

incredibly far away and in the way of its fulfillment lay unknown obstacles and dangers, endless weary miles and killing work. Well, that part of it was all behind him now. There might still be conflict, probably would be, to some extent. But the more important objectives had all been reached and conquered. It was good to be young and to know that you were going to live and grow with a young, new country. He took off his hat, tipping his face to the faintly stirring air.

He became conscious of a presence beside him and he turned quickly. It was Maidie Abbott. Her laugh was soft.

"Greedy! Wanted all the stars to yourself, eh? Well, Jumbo told me to tell you they were going to throw a little poker game, if you were interested."

"Not interested," said Dave. "Not now."

He watched her, standing there. Here, also, was a part of that young life he had been thinking of, a slim, gallant, very desirable part of that life. A certain recklessness washed through him. His hands shot out, catching her by the shoulders, pulling her close to him.

"You said something about the stars, about me wanting them all to myself," he said. "Well, you're right, Maidie Abbott. And the brightest one of all is you. And I want you, too. I've wanted you from the day I first laid eyes on you, when you looked like a rag-tag stripling, back along the Navajo River, as you and your dad argued with the Trempers about the use of the forge. I wanted you then, I've wanted you every day since then . . . and I want you now."

He drew her close to him, looking down into her still, upturned face. She was breathless, her eyes were wide and intent, as though she was searching, trying to read what was in his mind. It might have been the starlight, but her face seemed very pale.

Dave shook her slightly. "Do you hear me, Maidie Abbott?"

"Yes," she breathed softly. "Yes, I hear you, Dave. Is . . . is wanting me . . . loving me?"

His laugh was soft, almost fiercely exultant. He shook her again, slowly, powerfully, making her slim body rock from side to side. "Love you? Of course . . . of course. Like I love the night, the stars. Like I love the smell of wood smoke at twilight. Like I love blue distances and the far, lonely hills. Why, you're life to me . . . life!"

Her lips parted, working as though she would speak. Only, for a moment, she made no sound. Then her arms went up and around his neck. She clung to him.

"Dave," she said. "Oh, Dave, darling. . . ."

For one brief moment their lips clung. And in that moment a hard, remorseless pressure drove against the center of Dave's spine. And a thin, venomous voice smashed the glamour of the night. The voice of Lon Estes!

"You move or make a sound, Salkeld, and I shoot your spine in half. This is better luck than I dreamed. All right, Wolf . . . grab that girl!"

As Maidie gave back, startled, dumbfounded, an arm encircled her throat and a hard, brutal hand was pressed over her mouth. She was torn free of Dave's dazed grasp and dragged back into the darkness. Then, as a ripple of explosive fury swelled Dave Salkeld's muscles, something crashed down on his head, driving him from the night and stars, far down into a pit of roaring blackness.

At that moment, although Dave Salkeld did not hear it, there sounded, faint and flat with distance, from the basin above Painted Rock, a single gunshot. On the heels of that shot, a whole volley more, swelling and ominous.

CHAPTER NINETEEN

From the Flying Diamond cook shack, replete with food and with cigarettes going, the crew straggled over to the bunkhouse and had a look at Wampus, marking his improvement with nods of satisfaction. They gathered at the far end of the place. Jumbo broke out a deck of cards. "Come on, you hairpins," he challenged. "We ain't had one of our old-time stud sessions since we hit this new country. And I ain't forgetting that the last time we played, those two bottom-dealing slickers, Dirk and Pudge, kind of teamed up on the rest of us and robbed us of everything but our shirts. I been craving revenge ever since and tonight is the night. Gather 'round and take your beatings. I'm feeling lucky."

Dirk grinned. "You hear that, Pudge? The big Siwash wants to donate a few more *pesos* to us. Well, that suits me. I always did love to play poker with a gent who just can't get it through his thick head that two big pair don't rate shucks against three little deuces. The man is dumb, but he's asking for it. Come on, Buck . . . and you, Tonto. You might just as well get in on the skinning of that fat grizzly. How about you, Jim?"

Jim Abbott shook his head, chuckling. "I'll sort of look on. To be honest, I always had a weakness for two pair myself."

"Don't let 'em bluff you, Jim," rumbled Jumbo. "They ain't near as smart as they let on. When they win, it's only because they're drippin' with luck." Abbott chuckled again. "Well, in that case, maybe I will try a few hands. I can always. . . ."

He broke off, listening. "Hear that?" he exclaimed. "Gunshot. Sounded like it was up where the Pike boys are holding down that upper cabin."

They were quiet, listening. "There's some more," said Buck Custer swiftly. "Now . . . what the hell?"

He hurried outside, the rest following. The thin, flat echoes continued to roll, down from the country beyond Painted Rock. At intervals a heavier, deeper report broke through. "That's Ed Pike's old Forty-Five-Ninety bear gun!" exclaimed Dirk. "Buck . . . those boys are in trouble up above!"

"Converse!" gulped Pudge. "Maybe it's Converse . . . !"

Buck Custer cupped his hands about his mouth. "Dave! Oh, Dave!"

There was no answer. Buck called again. Only the faint echoes through the night answered him.

"I saw him last walking down by the corrals," said Jim Abbott. "And Maidie . . . Maidie was with him." Then he called—called both Dave and Maidie. But there was no answer.

Tonto Rice made a restless brushing movement of his hands past the guns on his hips. "Something is rotten about this," he growled harshly. "I've had a feeling all evening that Converse. . . ."

The rest of what Tonto was about to say was drowned out by the crashing snarl of a rifle from the ridge south of the headquarters. Something *hissed* over their heads and slapped heavily into the wall of the bunkhouse. On the heels of the shot, a heavy voice yelled: "Ride right through 'em! Clean 'em up!"

There sounded the concerted rumble of hoofs.

"Back!" rasped Buck Custer. "Into the bunkhouse! It's Converse!"

They sped for the bunkhouse, all but Jim Abbott, who stood momentarily frozen—thinking of his slim daughter. Where was she? What could have happened to her? She and Dave Salkeld couldn't have been far away. Yet there had been no answer to his call.

Behind him, Mose was calling from the cook shack. Jumbo answered, warning him. Mose headed for the bunkhouse.

The thunder of approaching hoofs finally jarred through Jim Abbott's indecision. But he did not head back for the bunkhouse. Instead, he crouched low and ran off to his right. As he did so, there came a *crash* of gunfire from the bunkhouse. Out in the blackness where those hoofs were racing in, a horse screamed with pain and a man gave a choked, dying yell. The night was torn wide open with the blasting fury of guns.

A charging figure, riding little wide of the main group, almost rode Jim Abbott down. He was past Abbott before he could shoot at that solid figure, crouched and moving. But the raider had glimpsed Abbott and now he set his horse to a rearing halt, spinning it on a dime, as he flipped his gun high in readiness for a chop-down shot.

Jim Abbott had no weapon—none but his brawny hands. He had no fear for himself—only a half-crazed worry for his girl. As the horse was whirling, Jim Abbott closed in with startling speed. He leaped high, gripped that gun arm, swung it over and back with a terrific wrench. The rider squalled with pain as he came out of the saddle in a heavy fall. As he struck the ground, Jim Abbott was on top of him, big hands driving deeply into the luckless renegade's throat.

The rider had lost his gun. He tried desperately, frantically to pull Abbott's hands free, but the maddened settler was merciless. Shortly the rider was limp.

Jim Abbott searched by feel for the rider's gun, found it, then went after the riderless horse, caught the trailing reins, and swung into the saddle.

There was nothing he could do to aid those beleaguered men in the bunkhouse, for the night behind him seemed filled with raiders. His girl Maidie? Something cold and terrible formed in Jim Abbott's breast. There was nothing he could do for her, either, and the conviction was upon him that some way, somehow, she and Dave Salkeld were in the hands of the raiders. Trying to locate them would be madness—suicide. There was only one thing he could do—one real stroke he could deliver, and he breathed a silent prayer that he would be in time. Jim Abbott set the nose of his mount downcountry, toward the silent stretches of Gallatin Basin.

Back in the Flying Diamond bunkhouse, the first flurry of excitement over the surprise attack subsided. Only by grace of that first shooting above Painted Rock had the whole outfit been saved from immediate annihilation. But now they were behind stout log walls and they had managed to do considerable damage to that first attacking charge.

Buck Custer called sharply to his men: "Don't waste lead, boys! This is liable to run out into a siege . . . a long one. They can't get at us in here and it'll be a bigger chore than they want to tackle to root us out. So save your lead until you're just about certain of making it good. We're damned lucky that we weren't caught flat-footed."

"Lucky . . . except for Dave and the girl," growled Tonto.

"Hold a good thought for them," said Buck harshly. "Maybe they're safe enough, hiding out somewhere."

"They must have got Jim Abbott," said Pudge gravely. "He ain't here. He was right alongside of me when that first shot came, but I lost track of him."

"I see'd somebody on foot, dodgin' off down crick, when I came gallopin' in from de cook shack," offered Mose.

"Maybe he lost his guts," said Pudge. "And coyoted on us."

"Hell, no!" boomed Jumbo. "Jim Abbott's as game a man as ever lived. Chances are he's trying to find his girl. I would . . . in his place."

187

Tonto, peering from a window, slid a rifle to his shoulder and fired. A wailing yell answered the shot. "Got him!" snarled Tonto. "They're trying to set a fire against the cook shack. I got him against the light."

"Fire," said Pudge. "That's liable to be bad."

"Forget it," rumbled Jumbo. "They can't burn us out. They're fools to try. All our buildings are new-built, out of green timber. We're sittin' snug. If it wasn't for Dave and the girl and the Pike boys up above, I'd feel like singing. Converse has bit off a mouthful that's liable to choke him before this hand is played out."

"Then you figure it's Converse?" asked Pudge.

"Hell, yes! Who else could it be? Not those night raiders that hit the settlers. We shot them to tatters. Ain't enough left of them to try an attack like this. And we know it ain't any of the settlers. We're in good with them. So . . . it must be Converse because it couldn't be anybody else."

"Lookit," mumbled Mose. "Tryin' to start that fire again." Mose had his old double-barreled shotgun loaded with buck-shot shells. He slid it over the window sill and let both barrels go. Two crouched figures, cursing desperately as they tried to get flames to bite into the solid walls of the cook shack, were blown down like leaves before a high wind.

Mose hunkered down in safety, sliding two fresh shells into the reeking tubes of his weapon. "Teach those no-'count scalawags to burn my kitchen," he growled.

The blast of death Mose had turned loose brought another furious volley at the bunkhouse, but the stout logs ate up the hostile lead.

"Me," said Dirk, "I cussed these logs plenty when I was cut-tin' 'em. But I bless 'em now."

The outside shooting slackened and a sort of stalemate set in, and the hours of the night began sliding away. Some shooting still sounded far up in the basin above Painted Rock and the occasional heavy *boom* of Ed Pike's big bear gun told the Flying Diamond boys that the fort was being held up there, too.

In time Jumbo became restless. Not a shot had been fired at the bunkhouse for over a couple of hours. "Maybe they've pulled out, given it up as a bad job," he growled. "I got a notion to go and see."

"You can shed that notion quick," rapped Buck Custer. "We ain't lost a man so far . . . and we're not going to, if I have anything to say about it. Converse sprung his attack a little off time. He's got a bear by the tail and knows it. We'll just sit tight and let him figure out the next move."

"But there's Dave and Maidie," argued Jumbo. "We don't know what happened to them. Maybe they're in a spot where a little bit of help will mean a lot of difference. And me . . . I'd like to have a try at finding 'em. If I could. . . ."

"No!" rasped Buck. "If I thought there was any chance of doing something for Dave and Maidie, we'd all go out and take a whirl at things. But we don't know where they are or how they are and we'd just be running around blind, fat meat for Converse's guns. Besides, Dave Salkeld ain't a fool. Neither is he a soft touch for any man in a row. Wherever he is, however he is, Dave is using his head right now. And we're going to use ours."

Mose, who had been listening carefully at a window, exclaimed excitedly: "Marse Buck! I jess heard that Converse coyote give an order. They got a log. They aimin' to bust down the door. They aimin' to come right in!"

Buck Custer did not argue. He leaped to the door, swung away the stout bars. "Over here with that shotgun, Mose! Quick! Tonto, come here with that Winchester. Ready, now. When I open it, give 'em hell. Then get back so I can close it again."

Buck Custer opened the door a trifle, eyes and ears straining.

It was black dark. But he could hear. Mumbling voices, *thud* of boot heel, scuff of spur chains.

Out there in the blackness there were eight men with that log, four on each side, holding it waist high. "All right," panted one of them, "let's go!"

Twenty yards away they were, starting at a walk, which quickened to a shuffling run. Buck Custer, unable to see a thing, heard them plainly enough and swung the door wide.

"Pour it to 'em," he growled.

At ten yards' distance the contents of both barrels of Mose's shotgun crashed into the luckless renegades. On the heels of this deadly hail came slugs from Tonto's snarling Winchester rifle, as he levered it empty. Buck Custer rolled both belt guns.

It was blind shooting, but it was terrific, just the same. The log hit the ground, sliding to a harmless stop. But the men who carried it were smashed back and beaten down. Six of them stayed down, two motionless, the other four rolling and twisting. The two unscathed survivors ran panic-stricken into the night. Not a single shot was fired in return before Buck Custer had slammed the door shut and dropped the bars once more into place.

"That's a chunk of music they don't want to hear over again," rasped Tonto. "That hurt."

When Dave Salkeld got his senses back, he found himself lying on the ground, tied hand and foot. At first the only thing he was conscious of was the thunderous agony in his head. Half conscious, he groaned. A hard boot toe drove into his ribs.

"Shut up!" rasped someone, cursing him. "You ain't begun to know what hell is. You'll die slow, with me remembering every punch you hit me with that day in town."

The thin, cold, merciless crackle of that voice cut through the fog of pain. Lon Estes.

"Your size, you dirty renegade," blurted Dave thickly. "Kick a man when he is tied and helpless."

The answer was another barrage of savage kicks and a thin, dreadful cursing. Dave's senses drifted away again for a time. But the natural strength and virility in the lean, rock-hard body welled up and his mind cleared.

"Come on, Estes," someone was growling. "We got to get down there and help Converse. From the sound of things, he's run into something he ain't cracking any too easy."

"It was those damned fools opening too quick on that line camp cabin up above," rapped Estes. "They were supposed to wait until they heard the shooting start down here, before closing in on that cabin. And by the sound of things they didn't make much of a surprise of that, either."

"I don't know a damn' thing about that . . . or care, either," spat the other. "All I know is we better get down there and help Converse. Else he's going to raise hell with us."

"All right," said Estes. "Skagway, you stay here with these two. Watch 'em as you never watched anything before. If they get away from you, I'll skin you alive . . . and slow."

The *thump* of hoofs sounded as Estes and his companion rode away. Dave's thoughts were working clearly again by this time. He had it all figured out. Estes, and the remnants of the outlaw gang, had tied in with Converse, and the combination had hit the Flying Diamond in an attempt to wipe it out. Apparently the try was not working out any too well.

The irony of his own position at this moment of need galled him mercilessly, yet he knew a swell of pride in his outfit. Tonto, grim and savage, a regular old he-wolf in a fight. Jumbo, big and boisterous, but afraid of nothing on earth—deadly and unstoppable as a grizzly bear when his dander was up. Buck Custer, his grizzled, quiet partner, staunch and true as steel. And the other boys, sound and game and trustworthy. Even

Mose could be a terror when he wanted to let go. Yes, there was good reason why Converse and his outlaw allies were having their troubles.

Dave rolled his head. "Maidie!" he called thickly. "Maidie . . . are you all right?"

Her voice was startlingly soft and clear. "Yes, Dave . . . I'm all right. And . . . I'm thankful to hear your voice. I thought you were dead when they brought us up here. You were so limp, so dreadfully limp."

Skagway, the renegade guard, spoke. "You two shut up. Shut up . . . else I gag the girl and kick your teeth in, Salkeld. You hear me . . . shut up! No more talking."

"I'll talk to you, Skagway," said Dave. "Name your own price and you can have it . . . if you'll cut me loose and give me a gun. And I'll keep my word. You'd be dealing with an honest man, not one of those whelps who would cut your throat and throw you aside, if the fancy struck them. Like Estes."

Skagway stirred slightly. "Not interested," he growled. "Shut up!"

"A thousand dollars," persisted Dave desperately. "A thousand in gold. All yours. You don't have to split with anybody. You can buy a lot of life with a thousand dollars, Skagway."

The fellow laughed harshly. "What good would a thousand or a million do me, with Lon Estes and Wolf Rossiter alive and knowing I'd sold them out? Hell, I wouldn't live long enough to enjoy a nickel of it. Not a chance, Salkeld . . . not a chance."

Dave realized this now. The fellow's fear of Estes and this Wolf Rossiter was far greater than his lust for gold. No use working on that angle any more. If he was to get Maidie and himself out of this jackpot, it had to be by some other means. He tried his bonds and found them savagely tight. But by the feel of them he knew what they were. Rawhide pigging strings.

"All right, Skagway," he said. "You know your own business. But I'll tell you something. In the watch pocket of my Levi's there are three or four gold double eagles. I'm telling you that because I'm so thirsty I could choke. How about a drink of water? And the lady . . . she could stand a drink, too, I reckon."

Skagway was silent for a time. Then Dave heard him stir and presently he loomed in the dark, swinging a canteen in his hands. "You try and pull any funny stuff and I'll stamp your face in," he growled harshly. "And if that money ain't there, I'll stamp it in anyhow."

"It's there," said Dave. "Try and see."

Skagway fumbled at the pocket and grunted with satisfaction as he brought out the smooth, heavy coins. Then he unscrewed the cap of the canteen and held it to Dave's lips.

Dave went at the water like a man dying of thirst, went at it so avidly that, with a sudden lunge of his head, he knocked the canteen from the fellow's grasp. Skagway stepped back, cursing. "All right, you damned greedy hawg," snarled the renegade. "Now you've spilled it. Go thirsty and be damned to you."

"Sorry," mumbled Dave, rolling half over. "Didn't mean to."

Skagway was pocketing the coins before he searched on the black earth for the canteen and in that moment Dave had pushed his bound wrists desperately toward the sound of gurgling fluid. He found it and felt the water from the canteen pouring over his hands and wrists—and the rawhide pigging strings. When Skagway bent to find the canteen, Dave squirmed slightly aside.

"Right alongside of me, sounds like," he mumbled. "Sorry I spilled it, Skagway. Give me another mouthful . . . please."

"Go to hell," growled Skagway roughly, jerking the canteen up. "Now shut up. Another squeak out of you and you'll be sorry."

He slouched a little distance away and soon Dave saw the red eye of a cigarette winking in the dark and smelled the tobacco smoke. Dave smiled to himself and sent a ripple of strength along his arms and wrists and felt the wet rawhide strings that bound him stretch appreciably. The game wasn't played out yet—not by a damned site.

Stalking back and forth in the dark beyond the Flying Diamond bunkhouse, Luke Converse was in a raging fury. From the first, this raid had backfired. Things had gone wrong up at the line camp cabin. The men he had sent in there to clean up that camp had blundered. Shooting had started up there prematurely, and that shooting had served to warn the main Flying Diamond crew just in time. He had lost men and that abortive attempt to batter in the door of the bunkhouse had raised hell with the morale of his outfit. When he tried, raving and cursing, to get his men to have another try with the log, they refused flatly.

"Not for me," growled one of them. "I'm willing to tangle in any kind of a reasonable fight. But that log business is slaughter, Converse. To hell with the log. Those *hombres* in the bunkhouse will be on the look-out for another try and finish it just like they did the first. Not for me."

Converse kept up his storming and cursing, but to no avail. From the confident, lustful crew that had ridden with him to the initial attack, his men had turned wary and reluctant, their confidence in their chances waning rapidly. To them it was beginning to look like a lost cause. Yet they were reluctant to give up. For every man jack of them knew they had started something that would not stop now until one or the other outfit reigned supreme in Gallatin Basin. Right now they had the Flying Diamond bottled up. But once that outfit got loose, where the odds were even, things would be wide open. Knowing this, the renegades hung around like a pack of prowling wolves, wary over attack, yet hating to let their prey escape. They were still in this state of indecision when gray dawn began to steal in out of the east. Then one of the renegades happened to look down the range toward the misty gulf that was Gallatin Basin, and what he saw left him momentarily stunned and speechless.

Up the creek they came, half a hundred men, some mounted, some on foot. A horde of settlers, with Jim Abbott and Dan Stinson leading them. True to their promise, the settlers had come to the aid of the Flying Diamond, in repayment for the aid the Flying Diamond had given them.

The renegade found his tongue. "Look!" he bawled. "Down-creek! Settlers! An army of them!"

Consternation greeted this announcement. The renegades who were still able to raced for their horses. From the mass of settlers a deep-toned shout arose. Men and horses came on at a run. Guns of all kinds began to roar. Winchesters, revolvers, huge old Sharps buffalo guns, shotguns, ancient muskets.

What it lacked in careful aiming, that fusillade of lead made up in density. Converse, staring for a moment like a man stupefied, died in his tracks, literally shot to pieces.

Slim Jepson, one of Converse's right-hand men, had died during the attempt to batter in the bunkhouse door. Bob Chehallis, deadly in a man-to-man fight, took two steps toward his horse before a slug from a buffalo gun knocked him spinning. Saugus Lee got as far as his horse and into the saddle. Then both he and his horse went down together.

Remaining renegades fled up toward Painted Rock, hoping to escape that way. But up at the peak of the Painted Rock trail, a bloodstained man with one arm hanging loosely had just stopped. It was Ed Pike. Clinging to his back, one leg dragging, was his brother Jerry. Ed Pike's face was gaunt and terrible from weakness and effort, as he dropped to the ground and let Jerry creep off of him. Both of them had belt guns. They rested a moment, looking into each other's eyes. Slowly they smiled, twisted, pain-racked smiles.

"I reckon Pap would have been right proud of us this night, Ed," said Jerry. "We sort of showed that the Pike blood breeds fightin' men. Looks like things are tightenin' up down below. Reckon we can throw a little more lead and bottle up this trail?"

"I reckon," said Ed. "Catch 'em on that open turn down below."

They did. Not a man or a horse got by that open turn in the Painted Rock trail. It was a bitter, savage, merciless thing that took place between the Painted Rock and the edge of Gallatin Basin, there in the growing light of a new day. But it marked the birth of justice through half a million roaring acres. It epitomized the terrible wrath of an aroused people against the lawless and the despoiler. That conscience that found itself in the hanging of the Tremper gang grew to its full strength there in the shuddering dawn. The fullness of complete law had come to Gallatin Basin.

CHAPTER TWENTY

At the first appearance of the settlers, two men had raced for the southern slope. On foot, they were less conspicuous than the renegades who had leaped for horses. They fled cunningly, taking advantage of each bit of cover, each swell of land. While men were dying under the guns of the Pike boys up there on the Painted Rock trail, Lon Estes and Wolf Rossiter raced over the top of the ridge to the south and into the timber beyond, where Skagway waited with horses and two bound prisoners.

"What's going on down below?" growled Skagway. "Sounds like all hell's broke loose. What . . . ?"

"Settlers," panted Estes thinly. "Damned sodbusters . . . looked like a hundred of 'em coming in . . . led by Jim Abbott. They've wiped out Converse and his crew. Quick! Those bronc's. We're traveling, and traveling far and fast!"

They threw Dave Salkeld and Maidie Abbott into saddles, then spurred away into the timber, racing south along the curving foothills, startling and scattering cattle that bore the Converse brand, cattle that had been destined to swamp the Flying Diamond range had their former owner been successful in this murderous night raid. But now those cattle were without an owner and most of them would go to fill the kettles of the hungry settlers of the basin.

Estes paid no attention to the cattle. His only concern was with his back trail and the trail ahead. He rode furiously, setting a breakneck pace. South to the split peak, then up the north cañon, while the horses foamed and gasped and the prisoners swayed desperately against their bonds, dazed and beaten by low-swung limb and dragging brush.

They stopped at last, in a clearing where the dead ashes of campfires marked their former camp. Estes swung down, snapping an order that sent Skagway riding into the timber. Rossiter sat his saddle, staring at Estes, who turned on him savagely.

"You, too!" shrilled the gunman. "Go help Skagway with those fresh bronc's."

Wolf Rossiter, his big, vulpine, bony face twisted and savage, shook his head. "The bronc's can wait," he growled. "Right now we're settlin' about . . . those two." He nodded toward Dave and Maidie. "What you figgerin' on doin' with them?"

"My business," rapped Estes.

"Mine, too," retorted Rossiter. "Because my neck and skin are concerned. It ain't going to take long for that fire-eatin' Flying Diamond crew to locate our trail and come foggin' along it. Which means that if we try and hang on to Salkeld and the girl, we're going to have blood-hungry riders on our trail if we ride a thousand miles. 'Specially because of the girl. Had we won that fight it would have been different. Then you could have hung onto 'em and done as you pleased. As it is, I'm all for turnin' 'em loose and clearing out of here for good. Skagway feels like I do about it."

Estes crouched slightly, his talon hands brushing back and forth across his guns, his face so thin and drawn with hate it seemed that the bones were about to burst through the tightly stretched skin.

"You're going to push yourself past the edge any second now, Rossiter," he gritted. "For that matter, I can't see you doing me a bit of good from here on out. You'll only clutter up my trail. You ain't an inch away from hell."

Rossiter's face paled slightly; he ran the tip of his tongue over dry, stiff lips. But he stuck to his argument stubbornly. "Skagway and me, we rode with you on this Converse deal," he croaked. "We stuck by you, Estes. We got a right to call for a square break. Maybe you hate this Salkeld's guts. But you got no right to expect Skag and me to risk our necks jest so you can satisfy that hate. And that girl. Why, every able-bodied man in Gallatin will be after us because of her. Like I said, it would have been different, had we won. But we didn't. Converse and his crowd are all shot to hell. Our gang likewise. Listen to sense, Estes. Turn them two loose and we get across the mountains."

Estes's head was swinging slowly from side to side, like a cobra about to strike. His voice was little more than a hissing whisper. "You going to help Skag round up those fresh bronc's?"

Desperation flared suddenly in Wolf Rossiter. "No, by Gawd, I'm not!" he yelled. And with the words he set his mount to rearing while his free hand lashed for his gun.

Three smashing reports echoed across the clearing. One from Rossiter's gun—two from the weapon that leaped into the hand of Lon Estes.

Dave Salkeld, watching the whole thing intently, saw a flutter of Estes's shirt as a slug plucked at a loose fold of it. He saw Rossiter, reared high and stiff in his saddle, beginning to lean far, far back. Estes's gun stabbed flame and thunder a third time and the impact of the slug drove Rossiter clear over the bunched haunches of his nervously plunging horse. Rossiter never moved after he hit the ground.

For a moment Estes stared at the fallen outlaw. Then he whirled, holstering his gun, and with quick, savage jerks freed the bonds that had held Dave's ankles fast to the cinch rings. He yanked Dave from the saddle, and Dave floundered clumsily as he tried to stand on feet that felt half dead and clubby from stricture. Then, without warning, Estes stepped forward and smashed him in the face with a venomous fist. Dave went down under the blow, blood running from his lips.

Maidie cried out: "You coward! You filthy, creeping, poisonous brute!"

Estes did not seem to hear her. He stood over Dave, lips pulled back from his teeth in a snarl of hate. "How do you like that, Salkeld? Just a little of the medicine you handed out to me in the Free Land Saloon that day. How do you like it?"

Dave, struggling up on one elbow, his bound hands knotted and white, spat in contempt. "Your hands weren't tied that day, Estes," he said hoarsely. "One thing I gave you credit for all along, despite the rest of your rattlesnake make-up. I thought you had guts. I see I was wrong. You're not the wolf I figured you. You're just all coyote."

Estes stepped forward, a boot drawn back.

Dave laughed at him. "Go ahead, kick me. I can't do a thing about it. It's quite the safe thing to do, you yellow rat."

Estes swayed back and forth, gnawing his lips until they bled. The man's fury was an ugly thing. His hands rubbed back and forth over the butts of his guns. Once he half drew one, and Maidie gave a little gasp. Then her voice came to Dave, pleading: "Don't say anything more, Dave, darling. He's crazy . . . out of his head."

Estes whirled and ran to her horse, began to fumble at the knotted thongs that bound her to the saddle. "Crazy, am I?" he gritted. "Well, crazy or not, you've found out something, you little fool. I told you I'd have you. I told you that."

Before Estes got those knots loose, some kind of a strange instinct warned him. He whirled and looked at the blank wall of timber into which Skagway had disappeared to round up the fresh horses running there. And then, crouched low and on foot, sliding both guns free, Estes ran for the timber edge. Now Dave, ear pressed to the ground, made out the *thud* of hoofs as horses came plunging through that timber.

Maidie's agonized voice reached Dave. "Your feet are free, Dave. Run for it! Oh, my dearest . . . run for it!"

"No," mumbled Dave. "This is a better way. I've been waiting for this chance."

Dave was writhing desperately as he lay there on the ground, jerking his wrists, one against the other with all his strength. From the moment when, far back on the timbered ridge above the Flying Diamond, he had managed to spill the water from Skagway's canteen over the rawhide that bound his wrists he had been working surreptitiously at those bonds. The rawhide, soaked with water, would stretch slightly. That had been Dave's gamble from the first. It had worked to some extent. He had won a little slack.

No longer were his wrists and hands like pieces of dead wood, immovably lashed together. His efforts and the slackening of the wet rawhide had allowed the blood to flow again and he had feeling and strength again in his hands and wrists. But they weren't free—yet.

Up and down, one against the other, he racked his bleeding, burning wrists, and all the time his eyes followed every move of Estes with desperate intensity. If this gamble did not work—he was done. He knew that. So long had Lon Estes nursed his black hate and thirst for revenge, the man was fairly unbalanced. Dave knew what it would be. Estes would beat him, torture him, then kill him. After that there would be no one to stand against Estes in defense of Maidie.

Dave gritted his teeth and poured every ounce of strength he had into the fight. Fraction of inch after fraction of inch, he jerked his right hand from the clinging, cutting grip of that slimy wet rawhide. He could feel his knuckles, the bones of his hands bunch together under the pressure. He felt the folded skin over his knuckles cut and break and the warm sliminess of blood begin to run. It was that blood that did the trick. One last mad pull and one rawhide withe slid free. After that it was simple.

Dave drew a long, shuddering breath and lay for a second with his eyes closed. Wave after wave of agony ran up his arms. It was as though he had broken something, or torn a ligament loose. But he was free and, over yonder, where Wolf Rossiter lay dead, were guns.

He rose to his knees. Estes was close against the fringe of timber now, watching like a hawk about to swoop. Half a dozen free horses sped out of the timber into the meadow. Behind them came the renegade, Skagway.

Dave heard the thin mockery of Estes's voice—as he called a single word: "Skagway!"

Dave knew what was in Estes's mind. Skagway was to go the same way as Wolf Rossiter had gone. That would leave Estes alone with his prisoners, to do with them as he willed.

Dave only dimly saw Skagway try desperately to swing back to the safety of the timber, while Estes's guns spat and spat again in their murderous song. He barely noted the luckless Skagway, mortally wounded, clinging to his saddle for a moment or two as he tried desperately to return Estes's fire for Dave was leaping toward the crumpled figure of Wolf Rossiter, staggering on feet still heavy and clumsy.

He saw the precious gun lying there in the grass, not a yard from Rossiter's lifeless fingers. As Dave's hand closed about the worn butt of the heavy weapon, a gasping sob of relief broke from his lips. He lurched to his knees, the gun stabbing out in front of him.

Skagway was down, his frightened horse spinning away into the clear. Estes, slightly crouched, was watching Skagway die. Dave sent harsh words across the narrow yards of meadow: "All right, Estes. This is it!"

Estes whirled toward that voice. For a split second he was

dead still, like a man who had seen an apparition. He blurted, almost stupidly: "You . . . you . . . how?"

Dave fired his first shot with desperate care. He saw a tiny puff of dust rise from the breast of Estes's shirt, saw the renegade gunman lurch and stumble. But Lon Estes was a mad animal this day and that madness kept him up. His guns spat at Dave, but that first mortal slug Dave had thrown upset the fine co-ordination of Estes's brain and hands. The lead went wild, and Dave, with the same care as before, fired a second shot. Estes spun around in a blind, hopeless circle and went down.

Dave dropped the gun and walked slowly over to Maidie's horse. Maidie was wide of eye, with cold tears running down her face. Her lips were moving but she made not a sound. When Dave finally had her free of the saddle, she slid into his arms, half fainting. Dave held her tightly and presently she began to shiver. Then a torrent of sobs shook her and she clung to Dave wildly, wailing like a hurt child.

"Steady," crooned Dave, his voice thick and tired. "Steady, sweetheart. Everything is all right now. Everything."

"I thought I'd die . . . I thought I'd die . . . while you were fighting those bonds and . . . and after that gun," she moaned. "Oh . . . Dave . . . if that . . . that animal had happened to turn and see you. . . ."

"But he didn't," soothed Dave. "His own treachery and bloodthirstiness beat him. The shadows are all gone, Maidie. We can go back to our Gallatin Basin . . . to the sun and the stars. We're out of the shadows, I tell you. And there is all of life ahead."

She quieted and he left her resting on the green meadow grass while he stalked about the triangle of death. Wolf Rossiter, Skagway, and Lon Estes. They, all three, had met violent death.

When he got back to Maidie, she had a brave, but tremulous smile for him. "I want to go home, Dave," she said. "To the sun and the stars you spoke of. There are things I want to remember, and things I want to forget."

Dave nodded, helping her into the saddle. He swung astride himself, and they headed down out of the mountains, their thoughts and hopes running out ahead of them, beckoning them on.

ABOUT THE AUTHOR

L. P. Holmes was the author of a number of outstanding Western novels. Born in a snowed-in log cabin in the heart of the Rockies near Breckenridge, Colorado, Holmes moved with his family when very young to northern California and it was there that his father and older brothers built the ranch house where Holmes grew up and where, in later life, he would live again. He published his first story—"The Passing of the Ghost"—in *Action Stories* (9/25). He was paid 1/2¢ a word and received a check for $40. "Yeah . . . forty bucks," he said later. "Don't laugh. In those far-off days . . . a pair of young parents with a three-year-old son could buy a lot of groceries on forty bucks." He went on to contribute nearly 600 stories of varying lengths to the magazine market as well as to write over fifty Western novels under his own name and the byline Matt Stuart. For many years of his life, Holmes would write in the mornings and spend his afternoons calling on a group of friends in town, among them the blind Western author, Charles H. Snow, who Lew Holmes always called Judge Snow (because he was Napa's Justice of the Peace in 1920–1924) and who frequently makes an appearance in later novels as a local justice in Holmes's imaginary Western communities. Holmes produced such notable novels as *Desert Rails* (1949), *Black Sage* (1950), *Summer Range* (1951), *Dead Man's Saddle* (1951), and *Somewhere They Die* (1955) for which he received the Spur Award from the Western Writers of America. In these novels one finds the themes so basic to his Western fiction: the loyalty that unites one man to another, the pride one must take in his work and a job well done, the innate generosity of most of the people who live in Holmes's ambient Western communities, and the vital relationship between a man and a woman in making a better life. His next Five Star Western will be *Longhorn Trail.*